CHERRY BLOSSOM

Cherry's narrow boat home is sinking and she's persuaded to stay in a chalet at the hotel where she works. Cherry is smitten with the rather distant owner, Oliver. And despite his cool and aloof manner, she has never felt such passion, even towards her ex-husband. Oliver's brother, Darius, is far easier company. Whatever happens, she will always put the welfare of her son, Jay, first. Who will Cherry choose?

PATRICIA KEYSON

CHERRY BLOSSOM

Complete and Unabridged

LINFORD
Leicester

First published in Great Britain in 2010

First Linford Edition
published 2011

British Library CIP Data

Keyson, Patricia.
   Cherry blossom. - -
   (Linford romance library)
   1. Single mothers- -Fiction. 2. Hotels- -
   Employees- -Fiction. 3. Hotelkeepers- -
   Fiction. 4. Love stories. 5. Large type
   books.
   I. Title II. Series
   823.9'2–dc22

   ISBN 978–1–44480–643–4

Published by
F. A. Thorpe (Publishing)
Anstey, Leicestershire

Set by Words & Graphics Ltd.
Anstey, Leicestershire
Printed and bound in Great Britain by
T. J. International Ltd., Padstow, Cornwall

This book is printed on acid-free paper

1

The pool of water bubbled its way up through the floor of her home as Cherry looked on in dismay. She'd known that the narrow boat was in bad repair, but had thought it would get her through another few months until she found somewhere more acceptable to live. Acceptable to her ex-husband that was, who felt it wasn't the right environment for his son.

She loved it on the river as did her eight-year-old son, Jay. Quickly grabbing a couple of pillowcases, she stuffed as many still-dry clothes and possessions into them as she could and hauled herself out of the watery cabin on to the towpath. She unlocked her bike from the side of the boat. Just as she was about to pedal off, a man in jogging gear came bounding round the corner. He was plugged in to his iPod and didn't notice her until it was too late.

'Watch out,' she shouted, as he nearly knocked her off balance.

He waved cheerily, not hearing her shouting, and continued on his way.

Cherry then pedalled furiously to the Oarsman Hotel, further up the river. It wouldn't do for her to be late for work on top of everything else. Her thick, unruly, dark hair streamed out behind her and her face grew red with the effort of going as fast as she could with a loaded basket.

'Sorry I'm late, Pat,' she panted as she hurtled through the staff door.

'You're not. You're on time. Calm down. Who's after you?'

'I've had a bit of a morning, that's all,' Cherry replied, running her fingers through her hair.

'You're going to need more of a make-over than raking your hand through that thatch. Go on,' she said, giving Cherry a nudge, 'clean up a bit.' Pat opened a locker. 'And you'll probably be better off with these.'

Cherry looked at the proffered soft, brown moccasins, then down at her own feet. She was still wearing her muddy Wellingtons.

'What would I do without you, Pat?' She smiled weakly.

'Come and have a cup of tea when you're ready,' encouraged her friend. 'We're not too busy this morning, but the new owner arrived last night so we'd better not hang about. And I'm not even going to ask what you've got in those.' Pat indicated the pillowcases with a shudder.

Ten minutes later, Cherry emerged from the cloakroom looking a different person. Her hair was captured in a bouncy ponytail, she was wearing a fresh mint green overall and her feet were dry and warm in the moccasins. 'Will I do?' she asked. She and Pat had grown friendly over the few months that Cherry had worked as a domestic assistant at the hotel.

Although Pat was the housekeeper, she was not at all bossy and the two enjoyed an easy relationship. 'How's Jay? He's not in any trouble, is he?' asked Pat, pouring tea into two mugs.

'No, he's fine as far as I know. He stayed at his friend's house last night.' Cherry settled herself in a plastic chair, then confided, 'The boat's on its last knockings as far as I'm concerned. It could be repaired at the yard, but I can't afford it.'

'But where will you live?' Pat gasped, unable to take it all in. 'How will you manage?'

'Now you know why I was so upset,' Cherry said, making a face. She took a sip of scalding tea, then said, 'And the social worker's meeting me here this afternoon. I couldn't bear it if she took Jay away from me.'

★　★　★

After lunch, Cherry hurried along to the seminar room to clear up. It hadn't occurred to her that it may still be occupied.

'Sorry, I didn't know you were still here,' she apologised. She didn't recognise the man standing there, she would have remembered him. In one long look she drank in his dark formal suit, set off with a snowy white shirt and gold tie. He looked tired, she thought, as his green eyes met hers. 'Shall I come back later?' she added. More than anything she hoped that he'd say yes. Her body had taken over. A whole jumble of activity churned her stomach and she had to make a real effort not to reach out and touch him. She was hooked.

His eyes roved over her as he asked, 'What for? What have you come here to do?'

'I was going to take these things back to the kitchen. Can I get you some fresh coffee? It was a long meeting, wasn't it?' Immediately Cherry knew she had said too much. It wasn't up to her to offer coffee or comment on time spent.

'If this was your hotel, would you make any changes?'

'Yes, of course,' replied Cherry

without hesitation. 'But I don't think you need my opinion,' she added tactfully.

'Can you spare a few minutes . . . ' He peered at her name badge. 'Cherry?'

'No, I can't,' Cherry apologised, thinking of the social worker's imminent arrival. She dashed for the door, hoping her pounding heart wasn't audible. She was unaware of the look of amazement on the face of the man occupying the seminar room.

★ ★ ★

To the people who knew Cherry, she was a hardworking, doting mother. She'd do anything to help or protect Jay. Very few knew that she had an ongoing battle with her ex-husband about what was best for their precious son. Cherry was in no doubt that Alan loved Jay just as much as she did, but he lived at the other end of the country and was often away a few days a week on business. If Jay lived with Alan, he wouldn't be with his father every day and Alan's new wife always put her own two daughters before Jay. On the other hand, what could Cherry offer apart from all the love she possessed for her cherished son? Now she couldn't even offer him a roof over his head.

As the clock ticked towards the expected arrival time of the social worker, Cherry was feeling jittery. Quickly running cold water over her face and tightening the scrunchie round her ponytail, she made her way towards the alcove in the corner of the bar to meet the woman whose appraisal could break her heart.

'Hello, Cherry.' Her voice was stiff as a board and very restrained.

'Hello, Mrs Talbot,' Cherry said, glumly. 'Shall I get some tea?'

'No, I don't think this will take long, do you?' Mrs Talbot was frowning over the top of her glasses. 'I came here past the river,' she continued, looking meaningfully at Cherry who blushed and sagged. 'What's happened to your 'home'?'

'It's sinking,' Cherry admitted. Out of the corner of her eye, she saw Pat approaching the table. What was she doing? She usually kept out of the way when Cherry had personal things to attend to.

'Cherry, here you are,' Pat called cheerfully placing a bunch of keys in her friend's hand. Then she turned to Mrs Talbot. 'The keys to Cherry's staff accommodation,' she explained with an indulgent smile. 'We always value our good workers here.'

She turned and walked away, leaving Cherry to recover quickly, slip the keys into her overall pocket and beam at her companion.

'So Jay and I will be living here. You can check up on us at any time.'

'I see,' said the social worker frostily, gathering her papers and stuffing them into her briefcase. 'Good afternoon.'

Cherry ran to find Pat. 'How can I thank you enough! Is it really all right if

8

we stay?' Pat nodded, her eyes shining. She had a soft spot for this lively woman and her son.

'We won't be any trouble, I promise. Which room have you given us? It doesn't matter at all, I'd be grateful for a bed in a cupboard.' Pat still didn't say anything. 'It isn't a cupboard, is it?' asked Cherry, her lips twitching. She delved into her pocket and pulled out the bunch of keys. 'Chalet Three? The self-catering places? But that's terrific, Pat. Those places are bigger than the boat and there's a separate bedroom and kitchen and everything.' She paused for breath, then asked, 'What does the management say?'

'That's the catch,' Pat confessed. 'I haven't told them.'

'Then what they don't know won't hurt them, will it?' Cherry felt uneasy.

'As you know,' continued Pat, 'number three's due to be renovated soon and has been empty for a week. As it can't be let out, there won't be any rent for you to pay.'

For Cherry to keep Jay, she had to have somewhere legitimate for them to live and it would only be a matter of time before that wretched Mrs Talbot found out that things were not as she had been led to believe, but for the time being, she was more than grateful.

Cherry had a good arrangement for the school run. She walked Jay and his best friend, Tom, to school in the mornings and Tom's mum, Hazel, met the boys after school and brought Jay to the hotel where he stayed until Cherry had finished her shift. Today, Cherry had mixed feelings as the time approached when she would have to break the news to Jay that their home was no more.

'Hi, Mum. How's the boat? Did you manage to pump out all right this morning?' he asked.

'It wasn't so easy today, Jay. The bilge pump wouldn't work because the water had spoilt the batteries. The hole must be getting bigger and I'm afraid the river water won. I'm sorry, but the

10

boat's sinking.' Her heart went out to her son. Hazel, taking in the situation, steered Tom towards the door.

'Where will we stay? Are we homeless?'

'We've got a new home here for the time being. Want to see?' Cherry took his hand and walked him through the staff room and across a paved area to chalet three. Making a big show of opening the door, she bowed and ushered her son inside.

'What do you think, love?'

'Wicked!' said Jay wandering from the sitting room, through to the bedroom, kitchen and bathroom.

'I thought you could have the bedroom and I could sleep on the fold-out bed in the sitting room,' replied Cherry, trying to be cheerful. For all its faults, the old boat had been their home for a while now and they were both going to miss it.

Jay jumped up and down on his bed and looked around. 'Where are the rest of my things? Will we be able to get them?' he asked anxiously.

'I saved what I could, but some of it was so muddy and drenched, I had to leave it. I'll go back later and see if there's anything else I can bring over. Now, what sort of a day did you have?' She watched as Jay held out his plastic folder stuffed with a reading book, spelling words and drawings. On the top of the see-through folder was a picture he'd drawn of their boat, *Dream Maker*.

'Can I stick this up somewhere, Mum?'

'Of course you can,' said Cherry, ruffling his hair. If they had to live apart, she couldn't cope.

* * *

Leaving Jay in the hotel lounge, Cherry pedalled back to check on the boat. Armed with black bin liners this time, she dropped easily inside the boat and gathered more of their possessions. When she had as much as she could reasonably carry on the bike, she made her exit. The bank appeared much higher up now as the ailing boat sank deeper.

'Need a hand?'

Cherry looked up and saw the jogger who had passed her earlier. Ruefully, she accepted that she did need help and grudgingly held out her hand. 'Not looking too good, is she?' said the stranger ruefully. 'Not that I'm any expert.'

'She's done for,' said Cherry, furiously hoping threatened tears wouldn't embarrass her. Rapidly changing the subject, she said, 'I know all the usual joggers along here. You're new.'

'I'm staying at the Oarsman, do you know it?'

'I work there. Nice meeting you . . . '

'Darius.' He smiled.

Cherry tried not to gape. 'Like in the Pop Idol programme on TV?'

Darius laughed out loud. 'I think my parents had the Persian Empire more in mind at the time.'

His laugh was infectious and Cherry found herself smiling, until she remembered that she'd have to call on the lock-keeper and ask his advice as to the disposal of the boat and its belongings. It wouldn't do for the possessions she couldn't rescue to be found floating up the river.

* * *

Having settled Jay for the evening, Cherry took a short walk down to the river. She breathed in the night scent deeply. The grounds of the hotel had seemed more inviting a few weeks ago when the cherry blossom was out, but soon the flower beds would be in full colour. Hopefully her life would blossom too, but at the moment it seemed unlikely.

'I think we have unfinished business,' called a voice.

'Who's that?' Cherry felt a thrill as she half recognised the tone of the man in the seminar room. As he came into full view, she felt the tremor run

14

through her body again.

'Working late, are you?' he asked.

'Just getting some fresh air before,' she hesitated, 'going home.'

He came and stood close to her, his citrus aftershave mingling with the other fragrances of the evening. As she looked at him a frown creased his forehead and he cocked an eyebrow.

'Sorry, did you say something?' asked Cherry, feeling enormously stupid, like a young schoolgirl.

'Earlier on you said you'd make changes to the hotel if it were yours. Tell me what they'd be.'

Cherry focused her attention on the question and the river. Anything to take her mind off this man, whoever he might be. 'Well, for a start, I'd include that.' She nodded towards the river. 'I'm sure people book into this hotel because of its name. They expect to have access to the river. It would be good to include boat trips, or a few little rowing boats that they could use to go along to the lock. A couple of chalets could be erected further down from the hotel, much nearer the river, for fishermen. The hotel could host special breaks, like murder mystery weekends, singles events, wine tasting. There's so much that could be done. It's a nice enough hotel, cosy, but a bit . . . ' Having let her imagination run away with her, Cherry realised just in time that she had said enough, if not too much. She looked up and then bit her lip.

'Look, I've been a bit less than frank with you. I'm Oliver Fingle, the new owner of the hotel.' He put out his hand and Cherry felt a tingle of delight as she shook hands with him. 'Anyway,' he continued, 'you were saying that the hotel was a bit . . . boring?'

The hotel may be, but its owner certainly isn't, thought Cherry, wondering if she'd voiced her opinion out loud. What was happening to her? She was normally so straightforward with her thinking. Deciding that she'd better leave before she said something she'd regret, she turned away.

2

Despite the comfort of the chalet, Cherry hadn't slept well. She was more used to the gentle rocking of the boat than she thought. Whenever she did close her eyes, all she saw was Oliver who seemed to be mocking her. She knew she had to be careful or he'd find out that she and Jay were living at the hotel. In the night, she'd got up and looked out of the window, surprised for a moment that there was no moonlight glancing off the river. All she could see was the large hotel looming close by. It seemed to her that the alarm clock buzzed her awake just as she had got back to sleep.

After taking Jay and Tom to school as usual, she returned to the chalet and set about sorting out the belongings she had salvaged. A knock at the door startled her.

'Sleep well?' asked Pat.

Cherry rubbed her face. 'Not really.' Then she smiled and said, 'Pat why didn't you tell me that the owner was a gorgeous hunk?'

'Didn't know you'd be interested,' replied Pat. 'He wasn't sure if he was going to take over the running of the hotel when his mother died. He didn't want the other members of staff to know he was coming which was why I didn't tell you. Be careful about the chalet until I've had a word with him.'

'I'll be all right. I'll make sure he won't know I'm here. Time for a cuppa?'

Pat looked at her watch. 'Okay, but I mustn't stay long. I came to let you know that Oliver's holding a meeting in the seminar room at eleven. Would you be an angel and sort it out. They'll only want coffee and biscuits, that sort of thing.'

'No problem. Come and have a look at the drawing Jay did of the boat.'

★ ★ ★

By mid-morning, Cherry had cleaned and aired the seminar room once more. It was rather a cheerless place, she thought, as she threw a spotless white cloth over a table in the corner and unloaded crockery from a trolley. She found herself counting the teaspoons in order to prolong her stay there hoping that Oliver would materialise. But time was getting on and she couldn't afford to draw attention to herself. All she need do now was collect the thermos jugs of hot coffee from the kitchen. When she returned with them, she was surprised to find the room occupied. She recognised the jogger from yesterday, but today he was dressed in a baggy blue shirt, tucked into navy chinos. With that colour combination, it was hard to dismiss his good looks as he surveyed her with his cobalt blue eyes.

'Hi there!' said Darius.

'You shouldn't be in here, you know,' Cherry said sternly, looking accusingly as he poured coffee for himself.

'I must have missed breakfast.' Darius grinned, making no attempt at looking at all ashamed.

'Well now you've poured it, could you take it along to the lounge to drink. There's an important meeting due to start here in a few minutes. She followed him back down the corridor and made sure he was installed in the correct room. Her face mellowing, she tossed a cellophane packet of crispy biscuits on the table in front of him.

He looked up, his eyes twinkling. 'What's that for?'

'You said you missed breakfast.'

As Cherry continued with her work she couldn't get Oliver Fingle out of her head. She felt an overwhelming attraction for him which she couldn't understand as usually she was so level headed. She hardly knew him. What she needed was a distraction from him and was relieved to be asked to go down to the kitchens to help Andre with the inventory of the ambient goods. There was just enough time before Jay came back from school.

Andre always made her feel welcome and the large larder packed with tins and packets of fascinating ingredients always delighted her. She raced around, dodging between the shelves quickly identifying items and calling out to Andre how many were left. There must have been a more economical use of time in doing these inventories, but Cherry loved it so much, she was quite happy for things to remain the same. The hotel was, as she had admitted to Oliver, a little old-fashioned . . . behind the times. Whatever did he think of her? She'd been told before that she opened her mouth without thinking. But, at the time, she'd had no idea that Oliver was one of the owners. She was surprised that a young man like Darius was staying here. She would have expected him to be at one of the more central hotels where there was a lot more going on. Just as she'd rounded up the last box of sugar sachets, she heard Pat call to her.

'Jay's home. No need to hurry, he's playing cards.'

Strange. Usually, Jay huddled into an armchair in the lounge and read his schoolbook until Cherry was free. Although anxious to greet her son, she knew Pat, who seemed to dote on him, would have given him a drink of milk or juice and a couple of digestive biscuits.

'That's the lot then, Andre. See you soon.'

*   *   *

Hurrying upstairs, she found that Pat was quite right. Jay was in his usual armchair and on the table in front of him were a pile of matches and a pack of cards. She heard him say, 'Twist,' just as she identified his opponent.

'Darius? I see you've met my son.'

Darius stood up, scattering cards and matches. 'I didn't realise. I thought this poor child had been abandoned.' He grinned, but the words stung Cherry and made her feel she'd neglected Jay.

She hurried round and put a hand on Jay's shoulder, not wanting to be over demonstrative in case she embarrassed him.

'Darius is teaching me pontoon, Mum. I'm getting quite good at it, I think we should play for money next time,' he said, indicating the pile of matches in front of him.

'Perhaps I should quit while I'm losing.' Darius smiled. 'Now that your boat's sinking, have you got somewhere to stay?' he asked.

'We're living here,' said Jay, still excited at their new home. 'It's a great place. Do you want to see it?'

'I think Darius must have things to do, Jay. And it's supposed to be a bit of a secret where we're staying.'

'Now you've got me intrigued. Why don't I get us a cup of coffee and you can tell me all about it.' Darius stood up.

'No, not for us, thank you,' called Cherry. 'I'm still officially at work for another hour and a half. I could be in deep trouble with the owner, so I'll keep a low profile, if you don't mind.'

Darius shrugged. 'Okay. Catch you later, Jay. I'd better go and practise.' Jay giggled as Darius sauntered off with a wave of the hand.

★ ★ ★

Cherry didn't work at the weekends because of Jay. The two of them rose late on Saturday and lazed around the chalet doing odd jobs. Jay lined up his toys and clothes in the cupboards in his bedroom and Cherry made a list of essential items which they would have to get at the shops in town later that afternoon.

'What would you like to do after lunch, Jay? Anything special?'

'Don't mind.' He lay on his stomach on the settee gazing wistfully into the distance. Cherry sat on the floor near to him and gently pushed the hair off his forehead.

'Shall we go down to the river, then?'

She watched in distress as his little face crumpled. Gathering him to her, she whispered, 'Poor old you. You're missing the boat, aren't you?'

Jay nodded furiously and pushed his head closer to his mother. 'Will we ever be able to go back, Mum?' he asked unsteadily.

'I don't see how. The boat's gone. I've arranged for it to be towed to the yard, but I can't afford to have it repaired.' She felt it best to tell the truth, even though it would upset him. If he found out later that she'd lied, he'd never forgive her. 'We can go along to the lock-keeper's cottage if you like, he'd let you open the lock if a boat came. Would you like that?'

'Yes, I would,' said Jay, brightening at the thought.

'Then when we've done the shopping, we could play cards,' said Cherry, looking at her son to gauge his reaction. 'I'd better put matches on the shopping list.'

3

What do you know about the owner of the hotel, Pat?' asked Cherry one morning during a coffee break. She hadn't been able to stop thinking about him and wanted an opportunity to talk about him.

'Oliver? He's a lovely man. I saw him quite a bit when he was younger, but he stopped coming to see his mother here. I think they met up in London occasionally although they didn't seem close,' said Pat putting her feet up on the chair opposite her. 'Didn't you call him a gorgeous hunk?'

'Umm,' said Cherry dreamily. Then she sat up straight and said, 'Yes, I did. What do you think he'd say if he knew I was living here?'

'Yes, my goodness,' cried Pat upsetting coffee over her cream blouse. 'I've been thinking about that. He's a bit pre-occupied right now, let's not add to his problems. Please, Cherry, just try and keep out of his way.'

Out of his way? That was the last thing Cherry wanted to do, but she could see the sense in it. Changing the subject, she said, 'I went over to the lock-keeper's cottage with Jay at the weekend. He's found someone who might be interested in buying the boat. I might as well give it to him as there's so much wrong with it.'

Pat put a sympathetic hand on Cherry's arm. Looking at her watch and standing up, Cherry said, 'It's the half-term holidays coming up soon. I'll be in touch with Alan and Jay might go there. So I may be able to do some extra hours.' She moved to the sink and ran some cold water onto a cloth. 'Here, sponge out that coffee before it stains.'

* * *

On her way back to the upper floor guestrooms, an office door was ajar.

27

Intrigued, she peeped in to see if it was occupied.

'Darius! You again. You seem to go everywhere you shouldn't. This room is staff only. Come on and then I'll lock it behind you.'

Darius followed her into the room, a playful grin on his lips. 'How's Jay? Still gambling?'

'Don't say that. I'm in enough trouble over how I look after him. I need someone on my side, not against me.'

'Want to talk about it?' Darius leaned carelessly against the door jamb as Cherry fished in her pocket for a master key. She looked at him with his smiling eyes and easy manner. If only she could be as relaxed as that, he seemed to have no worries. It would be good to unburden herself to someone, someone who wasn't involved.

Finding the key, she firmly shut and locked the door. 'I'd like to get things off my chest, yes. Would you mind?'

'Your place or mine?' He grinned.

'That's just part of the trouble,' sighed Cherry. 'But if I'm going to let you in on my innermost secrets, I'll have to know I can trust you.'

'The curiosity is killing me. Tell me, will you?'

After Cherry had done that, Darius asked, 'So, why is it a secret?'

'The boss doesn't know I'm there. This is strictly between you and me. Well, Pat knows and obviously Jay knows a bit, but it's not to be talked about freely, understand?'

Cherry glimpsed Oliver's tall figure before he was aware of her presence. Taking the opportunity to view him in repose, she was amazed at the impact he had on her. Her cheeks flamed red and her insides liquefied.

She hadn't felt like this about anyone before. It was like having a schoolgirl crush, but surely she should be well past feeling like that. Even when she was at her most romantic with Jay's father, she hadn't felt as physically affected as now.

'Pat said you wanted to see me,' she stammered.

'Good morning, Cherry.' He broke through her thoughts. 'Come on, this is a business meeting not a coffee break.' The flinty glint in his eye made him even more attractive to Cherry.

'So, tell me about it.' Oliver sat, barely able to suppress his impatience. But Cherry hadn't been listening.

'I . . . er . . . could you repeat the question?' she flustered.

'I said that I wanted to hear more about the things you'd do if the hotel were yours.'

'Do you? Why?' Cherry couldn't think how her inexpert views could be of interest to Oliver. After all he was the owner and must have his own ideas.

He stood up and fingered his tie. 'When you voiced your opinion it was as though you'd already given it thought and I wondered why. Also, you spoke with such passion.' He sat down opposite her and fixed her with a penetrating gaze, waiting for her reply.

'I think it's the river that makes me feel like that.' As she spoke, Cherry relaxed, wanting to share her enthusiasm with him. 'The water's so tranquil. Even though there can be evil undercurrents, the flow of the water is peaceful. The swans float by and visit. There are birds and wild-flowers. You notice the seasons quite distinctly. The fishermen are part of the scenery, the river people are friendly . . . ' There was a prolonged silence after she tailed off. Cherry was embarrassed. She'd said too much again. She risked a look at Oliver. To her consternation, he gazed at her, but said nothing.

'Well, you did ask,' she said, rising.

Oliver put out a hand for her to remain. 'I didn't mean to be rude. Let me ask you something.'

Cherry smiled ruefully and sat back down. 'You want to know more?'

'Yes. I want to know if you'll work for me.'

'I already do,' Cherry said sharply.

'I mean in an advisory capacity. What do you do now? Cleaning? Something like that?' he asked in a dismissive tone.

'You'd soon notice if it wasn't done,' retorted Cherry stiffly.

'Yes, of course,' he replied impatiently. 'I understand it's important, but I'm talking about something else. I'm offering you a job advising me what you consider guests want from this hotel.' He smiled at her for the first time and her heart leapt. She found herself grinning inanely back at him. 'You'll consider it, then?' he asked.

'Yes.'

'Just like that? Aren't you going to ask about hours and pay? Or conditions of work?'

'I didn't realise this was an interview.' Then a thought struck her. 'Is it extra money, then? What's so funny?'

This time, Oliver's laughter rumbled out infectiously and Cherry joined in.

* * *

'I can't turn it down, Pat. I need the money. But how I'm going to fit it all

32

in, goodness knows.'

'If I can help, I will,' said Pat.

Cherry put an arm around her friend. 'Thank you. It means a lot that you've said it, but I must be able to be here for Jay. He's my responsibility.'

'Yours and Alan's,' replied Pat.

Cherry stared at her, her eyes wide. 'I'm surprised he hasn't been in touch. I wonder why I haven't heard from him.

'I'll ring him tonight. It will please him that we're not living on the boat anymore. Jay can speak to him as well. Thank you, Pat.'

★   ★   ★

After speaking to Alan and arranging for a delighted Jay to spend his holidays with his dad, Cherry and Jay went for a walk along the riverbank. Andre had given them some stale crusts and, although it was past their usual feeding time, a few ducks and birds paddled over to them and pecked at the bread Jay offered.

'I miss the birds, Mum.'

'But you are happy in the chalet, aren't you love?' asked Cherry.

'S'pose so. I don't really mind where we are. Can we call on the lock-keeper? I did a drawing for him at school.' Cherry watched as he carefully pulled out a folded sheet of paper from his pocket. She was caught in a flood of love as she bent to hug him.

'Careful, don't scrunch it up,' he said, hastily pecking her cheek.

4

Having answered the phone in the bedroom she was cleaning, Cherry was surprised to hear Pat say, 'Found you at last! Oliver wants to see you in his office, now. You'd better leave what you're doing. If you don't have time to finish I'll give you a hand later.'

Cherry couldn't think why Oliver would want to see her so urgently unless he knew about the chalet. With a sinking feeling she said, 'He's found out, hasn't he? Oh, Pat, what will we do? I'll lose my job as well as our new home. And you'll be in trouble.'

'He didn't look very cross when I saw him. He was practically dancing down the corridor when he asked me to find you. Then I heard him singing.'

'That's a relief. Maybe it's to do with this new role I'm supposed to have. Can you imagine me being his adviser?'

'Yes, but for heaven's sake stop talking and go to see him.'

Cherry giggled. Wait until she told Alan. His new wife was high flying, something to do with equity which she, simple Cherry, would never be able to understand. Alan was always shoving it down her throat. How clever Imogen was, how much money she made. She pushed the vac to one side, tidied the cloths she'd been using, then checked the mirror.

That morning she hadn't had time to do anything with her hair except quickly run a brush through it and tie it back and she looked rather pale. She pulled out the scrunchie, fluffed up her hair, then rubbed her cheeks to give them a bit of colour. Quickly she smoothed down her overall before heading out of the room to run down the stairs. In reception she noticed some petals had fallen from a rose in an arrangement onto a polished table. She stopped to bury her face in the bunch of roses and breathe in the scent, then quickly swept the fallen petals into her hand before dropping them in the bin. She liked things to be ship-shape. She'd always felt at home on the boat.

Oliver was busy at his desk. 'Have a seat, Cherry. I'll be with you in a minute.' Cherry had a chance to admire his broad shoulders and strong hands and wanted more than anything to walk round the desk and be taken in his arms. Gazing out of the window she imagined the two of them, their arms entwined strolling by the river, then sitting beside it and dangling their feet in the water. The sun would be shining and he'd throw back his head with a roar of laughter. Or they'd sit on the grass under the big willow and share some bread, cheese and wine. They'd clink glasses and drink to their future. Then they'd lie close together on the grass looking up at the patterns made by the sun on the leaves.

'Cherry?' Oliver was looking puzzled. 'You were miles away.'

'Sorry.' He certainly wouldn't want

to employ a daydream like her. She tried to look attentive and intelligent. Maybe Alan had been right when he'd told her during one of their rows that she'd never make anything of herself.

'I wanted to talk to you about the conference.'

'Conference? What conference?'

''Making the most of your situation'.'

Yes, she could certainly do with some help there.

'It's ideal for us. I've just booked two places. It should help us work out exactly how to make the best use of the river and the other amenities in the grounds. I've been thinking we could have crazy golf. I was also wondering about pony trekking along by the river. Perhaps you could check out the local stables. See what they have to say about that.'

Cherry hastily scribbled on the notepad he'd pushed towards her.

'We also need to find out about fishing rights on this stretch of the river. If we take a few ideas with us we can see what the experts think. We're off on Monday and we're going to be away three days. I have an itinerary here and all the talks and workshops look useful. There are also a couple of tours to places of interest and there's a boat trip which I think we should go on as you're so keen on rivers and water. And there are some motivating after dinner speakers too. There may even be dancing into the early hours.' His green eyes twinkled. 'That's the plan then, if you're willing to go.'

Willing? Willing to go dancing with Oliver? She couldn't wait, but she'd need to sort out some clothes first. She could hardly attend a conference in her overalls or jeans. She'd have to go to that cheap shop in town and see if there were any suitable bargains. Maybe she could cadge a lift with Andre when he went in to the market. Looking across the table at Oliver the thought of spending three days with him made her head swim. She really felt she should pinch herself to make sure she was awake.

'Are you okay? You look a bit pale. I imagine you've got someone to look after your son.'

'He's going to stay with his dad for the half-term holiday so that's perfect timing. Where is the conference?'

'Central London. We're staying in a luxury hotel so that should be an eye-opener too!' He chuckled. 'This place is a bit run down, don't you think?'

'Well, I wouldn't say that exactly.'

'Oh, yes you would, Cherry. I'd like you to be totally honest with me. We're going to be working very closely together in the future. There are going to be quite a few changes round here. I thought we'd start on a programme of redecoration. The first thing I'm going to change is this room. These frills and flounces aren't really me. Are you any good at that sort of thing? You know, colours, textiles?'

So she was going to be an interior designer too. Was there no end to her potential? She couldn't help but compare Oliver's positive attitude to her with Alan's negativity.

'Let's have some coffee,' Oliver said.

Cherry was about to stand to pour the coffee, but Oliver was already at the side table a milk jug in his hand.

'White? There's a lot I don't know about you, Cherry,' but he really wanted to get to know her better. Since meeting her in the seminar room he'd been unable to get her out of his head. He went to sleep thinking about her and his first thoughts of the day were about her. He was finding concentrating difficult. He wanted to take her in his arms and run his hands down her back, feel her body against his, kiss her face . . .

'Oh, Oliver, you've split the coffee.' Cherry was by his side, mopping at the tray, efficient as ever. 'Here let me.' She handed him a cup and saucer and he carefully made his way back to his desk. Of course, he was very emotional right now with all the changes that had taken place and the decisions he'd had to make, but even so his feelings were overwhelmingly powerful. They sat in silence for a while, each sipping their coffee, each lost in their own thoughts.

'He seems a nice boy, your son,' Oliver said to break the silence. He hadn't seen much of the boy, but he'd been quiet and well behaved when he'd glimpsed him now and then round the hotel. 'Does he go to the local Primary school?'

'Yes, and loves it.'

'They say schooldays are the best of your life. They weren't mine.' He hadn't meant to bring that up as he didn't want to sound as though he had a lot of baggage from the past. She was looking at him sympathetically so he went on, 'I was sent away to boarding school when I was eight. My father left us and my mother was busy with the business. Neither of them had time for me.'

'I'm so sorry, Oliver,' Cherry said.

'My father had a new wife and it wasn't long before he had a new son too. He wasn't sent away to boarding school. He had pretty much everything I didn't have, including my dad.'

Cherry's thoughts immediately turned to Jay and Alan. She blamed herself. If she'd been a better wife Alan might not have gone off with Imogen, they might still be together. But on the other hand if they'd stayed together and been unhappy and forever arguing it wouldn't have been any good for Jay.

'I hated boarding school,' Oliver said vehemently.

She couldn't see that boarding school had done him much harm, but it was a world away from the state comprehensive she'd attended in a rather run down city area. She'd hated living there and had longed to escape to the country. Perhaps that's why she'd married Alan. He'd simply offered her a different way of life. It may not have been the happiest of marriages, but Jay had been the result and she wouldn't be without him for anything.

Oliver was watching her closely as

different expressions fleetingly crossed her face. He hadn't met anyone like her before. She was so full of energy and so eager to try things.

She leaned across the desk to take his empty cup just as he stretched out his arm to reach for the itinerary. Their hands touched and they both jerked back as though electricity had surged between them. Oliver caught her glance which seemed to question his reaction.

Quickly clearing his throat he said, 'I'll copy the itinerary and booking form for you.'

She nodded.

'You'll see I've booked two superior rooms next to each other,' he said trying to sound business-like.

'Good, that's good,' Cherry said rubbing her hand as though it was raw from their contact. 'If that's everything for now I think I'd better go. I've still got five more rooms to clean and I'm a bit behind.'

'I need to work out a timetable for you if you insist on doing two jobs.

Perhaps you could spend a couple of hours in the afternoon on your new role and clean in the morning. I'll set up a desk in here for you. There's plenty of space. Would that suit you?'

'Yes, of course.'

She'd never appeared to be lost for words before and Oliver wondered if he'd offended her in some way. 'Shall we shake on the deal,' he reached out his arm. When their hands touched he felt the softness of her skin and couldn't resist caressing the back of her hand with his thumb. He was pleased when she didn't snatch her hand away, but lingered in his grip.

'I'm going to enjoy working with you, Cherry,' he told her, 'I think we'll make a good team.'

He wanted to pull her close and kiss her tempting lips, but instead gently loosened his hold and watched as she walked out of the room leaving behind a faint scent of summer and flowers

5

'You've always let us down,' cried Cherry. 'You're not the one who has to explain it to Jay. Let me know when you can see your son.' Cherry threw the phone back on the rest and put her head in her hands. Poor Jay. He'd be so disappointed that he wouldn't be seeing his dad over the holidays. She drew an exasperated hand through her hair and took a deep breath. As she did so, she remembered, almost as an afterthought, that now she wouldn't be able to go to the conference with Oliver. Disappointment washed through her. But that was a secondary consideration now. She hurried off to find Jay. He was in the staffroom chatting to Pat.

'Jay love,' began Cherry, 'your dad's just phoned. I'm so sorry, but he won't be able to have you there next week. He's double booked some sort of arrangements and can't get out of it. I'm sure he's as upset as you are.' Cherry looked over Jay's head at Pat who was screwing up her face in irritation.

'Dad works hard, doesn't he, Mum?' said Jay, trying not to look sad. 'But I don't mind being here with you and Pat especially if Darius is around. Can I go and look for him now?'

While Jay pottered off, Pat pulled out a chair for Cherry. 'Come on, get it off your chest. You look as if you're going to explode.'

With a huff, Cherry sat down. 'Alan hasn't got work commitments at all, Pat. Imogen and he are going to her sister's in Scotland and there isn't room for Jay. Why couldn't Imogen have taken her girls up there and left Alan to have Jay at home? They're so selfish.'

'You've always said that Alan dotes on Jay,' answered Pat, helping herself to a shortbread finger from the ever present biscuit tin.

'He does,' insisted Cherry. 'He's

always made time for Jay when he could. I know he works hard, but . . . Do you think it was wrong of me to imply that it was work stopping Jay going to his dad's?' Cherry nibbled a nail as she wondered about what she'd said.

'What will you do about the conference, now?' Pat always got straight to the point.

At the thought of missing out on her imagined wonderful time with Oliver, Cherry felt sick.

'Are you all right, Cherry? You're miles away.'

'But I won't be, will I,' wailed Cherry. 'I'll be here and . . . '

'I see. Are you attracted to our new owner?' Pat now gave Cherry her full attention.

'Of course not,' replied Cherry, fully aware that her face was the same colour as her name. 'I just hadn't made any arrangements to entertain Jay during the hols, that's all. I'll get some books from the library and there're bound to be some games in the lounge. There's always Darius. He plays a mean game of Pontoon apparently. Jay's completely hooked.' She babbled on unaware of Pat's smug smirk.

'You know I'll help out if I can. Jay's no trouble, but it's a bit difficult when I'm called away,' said Pat.

'Pat, you're always so good to both of us. I can't expect you to look after Jay and do your work. I'm sure I can arrange something, he's my responsibility after all. But, you're right, I won't be able to go away and that's flat. I'll have to tell Oliver I suppose, but he's not going to be pleased. I'll probably lose my job before I've started it. Just as well I didn't go clothes shopping after all.'

'You don't think Alan and Imogen are going through some crisis, do you?' asked Pat suddenly. 'And he feels he has to be with her now to sort something out.'

'You've been reading too many romances, Pat. I don't know much about his relationship with her. I've always imagined that she pulls the strings, especially the purse ones, but I've never been that interested enough to find out.' Cherry sipped at her cool tea. 'I wouldn't like him to have a bad relationship. Just because we didn't get on, I wouldn't ever begrudge him any happiness.'

'That's because you're a kind, sweet girl.' Pat went over and hugged a miserable Cherry. 'Why not stay here and have a fresh cup of tea. Give yourself ten minutes to relax.'

Left to herself, Cherry was ashamed that her first thoughts were for Oliver. On reflection, she knew Jay would be all right with her around the hotel for the half-term week — they'd done it before. He was a self-contained lad and, although always hungry, was content to entertain himself when he had to. But that was before she'd taken on these extra responsibilities. Perhaps Oliver wouldn't mind if Jay sat in the office with her when she was working during the afternoons. Darius, of course, was a bonus now. But how long would he be staying? If only she had some family. Then it hit her, was that why she resented Alan? Was she jealous of his family life? But who'd want her, coming as she did with Jay and no home? The thought of having someone like Oliver to share her future with was so very appealing. No, she was wrong there, she admitted to herself. What she really wanted was Oliver, not someone like him. Quickly, she wiped the thoughts from her mind. There was no chance of that now. She'd already let him down and she was sure he wouldn't forgive her. Besides, he deserved someone who would be an equal partner in every respect.

With a sigh, she realised she'd have to confront him and let him know she wouldn't be going to the conference. But try as she might, she couldn't drag herself from the chair and out into the reception area.

Cherry looked up guiltily as the door swung open and Pat poked her head in.

'Have you told him yet?' she demanded.

'Please don't nag, Pat, I'm just searching for the right words.'

'I can't go to the conference. Would they do?' smiled Pat. 'Go on, Cherry, you've got to let him know. Don't put it off any longer.'

Cherry stood up, took her cup to the sink and spent a few moments washing it, drying it and replacing it in the cupboard. Then she put the lid on the biscuit tin and put that away, too.

'Are you going to spring-clean in here before you speak to Oliver?'

'I think I'd like to. That cupboard looks as if it could do with a good scrub,' waffled Cherry.

Pat reached behind Cherry's head and took the scrunchie out. 'That's a bit smarter. You look less like a cleaner now.' Then she led Cherry by the hand to the door, opened it and gave her a little push. 'Go on, get this over and done with.'

Cherry wandered slowly through the hotel. Half of her couldn't wait to see

Oliver again and the other half wanted to be a long way away.

She heard him before catching sight of him. Roused by the sound of his voice, Cherry stayed out of sight, listening to his honeyed tone. It was mesmerising. She hadn't realised before how enchanting a voice could be. Without being able to hear Oliver's exact words, she knew by his gentle pitch that he was giving reassurance. A gentle laugh indicated that the conversation had reached an amicable conclusion and, sure enough, the guest he had been talking to gave an audible 'Thank you so much'. Before Cherry could stop herself she hurried forward intent on speaking with Oliver.

'Ah there you are Cherry. That guest,' Oliver nodded in the direction of the man in question, 'was asking if we had any river trips. I told him our chief executive for new projects had it at the top of her list and by the time next year's brochure comes out, we'll have the river included, plus a lot of other events and activities as well.' Cherry was aware of Oliver looking at her. The look on his face was surely more than one of an employer to an employee. But Cherry had to rid herself of all such thoughts and get on with her confession. She opened her mouth, but no words would form themselves.

'Right, Cherry, come along, there's work to do. Have you finished your morning duties? Are you an executive now?' His eyes sparkled at her.

Cherry gave a dejected nod, unaware how attractive she looked with her thick curls bouncing around her head. But Oliver had noted it, as he seemed to note everything about her. He knew that now was not the time to dwell on things of a personal nature. With luck those things could be taken a stage further at the conference during the leisure time he was looking forward to spending with this dazzling woman in front of him.

At the hastily arranged office desk, Cherry sat with paper and a pen in front of her. She started a list of the facilities she would like to have at a hotel if she booked into one. The telephone rang and Cherry automatically answered it.

'It's for you, Oliver,' she said, keying in his extension so that he could answer it at his desk. 'Duncan and Duncan, solicitors.'

'Oliver Fingle. Yes, Mr Duncan, I did want to speak to you about her.' He looked furtively at Cherry who immediately stood up and let herself out of the office.

Although Cherry was pleased to have been given a little grace before confronting Oliver, she was nosily wondering who he wanted to talk about so secretly. Why would a solicitor ring him? Then it struck her? It must be a personal crisis. A divorce, separation, maintenance or something like that. Well, she was blowed if she was going to be a second hand rose. Then a guilty thought crossed her mind that it could be something to do with his mother's will. Anyway, whatever it was it was nothing to do with her and she had a job to do.

Having brought the pad of ideas out of the office with her, Cherry perched on a chair in the corridor and finished the list. Something for the children to do, special meal events including perhaps a pudding club, speakers for leisure pursuits, a crèche. She then added that these facilities would be in addition to the outdoor ones already discussed, drew a thick line under it and decided that when she gave it to Oliver that would be the end of their management association.

Oliver came out looking for her. 'You needn't have vanished. I could have rung them back. But thank you.' He disappeared back into the office, then poked his face out again. 'Aren't you coming? There's lots to do'

Cherry held out the list to him. 'Here, I've done my best. That's all I can think of.' Oliver took the proffered paper and scanned it. 'Fine. Looks good. You could have the computer and type it up and save it in your file.'

Back in the office, Cherry fidgeted with the computer, pressing buttons and wiggling the mouse around. Then she took a deep breath and said, more loudly than she meant to, 'There's something I've got to tell you.'

6

Mmm?' Oliver seemed distracted. She wondered if he had even heard her. 'Hold on, I need to check something.' And he was gone. Abandoning all the paperwork, Cherry hurried after him and waited for his attention at reception. Finally Oliver looked up from the guest book. 'Something to tell me?'

Cherry couldn't believe she had to do this. Who in their right mind would cancel three days away with this gorgeous man? She gulped and wondered if he would be as bothered as she was to miss the opportunity of being together. Opening her mouth, she jerked out, 'I can't go on the conference, I'm sorry.'

Oliver seemed to sag visibly, then bracing his shoulders walked over to a group of chairs and gestured at a chintz settee. 'Come and explain. I'm sure we can sort something out. If there's one thing I've learnt it's that problems are rarely insurmountable.' Cherry tried to settle herself on the settee, but with Oliver's unsettling presence, she couldn't relax.

'Jay's father won't have him now,' she blurted out as she sat on the edge of the settee.

'Won't have him? But that's unforgivable. He's the boy's father and he promised.' Oliver stood looking down at her, his fists clenched.

'His name's Jay not the boy,' Cherry said crossly. She was disappointed about the conference, but felt that Oliver wasn't thinking of Jay's disappointment, more his own concerns about the hotel. Perhaps he wasn't the man she'd thought, but then she realised she'd done exactly the same thing in putting her feelings before Jay's.

'Couldn't someone else do it?' Oliver asked, his mood lightening. Cherry had already given a good deal of thought to this. She considered it again, but still came to the same conclusion that there was no one.

Deliberately misunderstanding Oliver, she said, 'Yes, someone could take my place. It's a pity Pat can't go. I'm sure she'd learn a lot and enjoy it. But she can't leave her husband for long. You must know Maurice has been ill.'

'I mean someone else can look after the . . . Jay. There must be someone you can ask.'

Cherry tried to think if there was anyone else she could ask. Hazel's family were going away for the week and she didn't want to leave Jay with anyone they didn't know well.

'I don't believe there's no one else.' Oliver sounded exasperated. 'Haven't you any family?' He moved away ready to get on with the next task on his list.

'No and I can't think of anyone else. I'm sorry I've let you down, Oliver, but you must realise how difficult it is being a single parent. If you want to think again about whether or not I'm suitable for the job I'll understand.' She stood up abruptly and turned to leave.

Oliver suddenly grabbed her arm. 'No, don't go. I mean . . . let's sit down and talk this through. Sorry, I've been pre-occupied. Please.' He gestured for her to sit down, then sat opposite her. 'I'd been so looking forward to a few days away with you . . . I mean planning things for the hotel, having time to talk about the future. It's always so busy here. I do realise how difficult it is for you, but please give this job a go. It's not a big deal; I expect there'll be another conference soon. The thing is I really think you can make a difference to the hotel. We'll be a great team.'

Cherry imagined them as a team, but her imagination took her beyond the hotel. She wasn't sure she ever wanted to marry again, but to have someone to share things with would be wonderful. Cherry could think of nothing more she'd prefer to do than spend time with Oliver. Her thoughts overtook her as she envisaged an evening wrapped in his arms ... Suddenly Pat appeared bearing a tray with tea and cakes.

'Thought you'd appreciate this,' she said carefully placing the tray on the table.

'I'll pour,' Cherry said quickly, glad to have a distraction from all her steamy thoughts.

'What do you fancy? Chocolate éclair, vanilla slice or Eccles cake?' Oliver asked.

As soon as she'd said chocolate éclair Cherry knew she'd made a mistake. Biting into the pastry, thick cream oozed out, but thankfully she managed to finish without making too much mess. She was starving and the cake had hit the right spot. For a split second she didn't care what Oliver thought of her, then she remembered her manners and swallowed hard. 'That was good,' she acknowledged, wiping her mouth with a napkin.

'I can see that.' Oliver laughed, then reached across and wiped her cheek gently. 'It's probably a good job I can't take you to the conference.'

Cherry felt embarrassed, but was happy to see that he was chuckling.

'Maybe we should have dinner together, spaghetti followed by Mississippi Mud Pie. Actually that's not a bad idea. How about this evening? We could bounce a few ideas around. What do you say?'

Was that how Oliver viewed her, Cherry wondered — like a kid who needed to be taken to the tuck shop in order to be softened up before getting on with her homework? Indignantly she opened her mouth to protest before realising that he was asking her to spend some time with him. This evening! Of course she realised it was only a work meeting.

What Cherry wanted to say was 'yes please' but she had Jay to think of. 'I'm sorry, there's Jay.'

Oliver looked disappointed. 'Couldn't he be left for a couple of hours?'

Cherry wasn't sure if he was joking and didn't reply. They sat in silence.

'You two look gloomy. What's up?'

'Cherry is absolutely adamant no one else can care for her son.'

'What's this all about?' Darius asked as he threw himself on to the settee next to Cherry. 'You're looking stressed, Oliver, and you look as though you could strangle him.'

'You'd be stressed if you had half my problems,' Oliver said sullenly.

Cherry felt even more uncomfortable now. Darius was a guest at the hotel, but was on first name terms with Oliver and the two men seemed over familiar with each other. Cherry briefly explained the difficulty of not having anyone to care for Jay. 'I don't think Oliver quite understands about looking after children.'

'Well, let's just say he has a somewhat distorted view.' Darius sat effortlessly, his legs crossed, a smile on his face. 'Any tea left in the pot? I'll use Oliver's dirty cup. Ah, cream cakes.' He helped himself to a large vanilla slice, licked at the icing, then took a large bite spraying crumbs everywhere.

Cherry was pleased to see that Darius was making even more mess than she had. 'Here let me,' she said wiping cream from his shirt.

'Oh, for goodness sake,' Oliver said crossly, glaring at them.

Cherry felt embarrassed, but Darius didn't seem to take any notice, he just carried on eating after giving Cherry a big wink which made her giggle.

'We're like brothers, Jay and me. Well, maybe not because we do get on well. I've taught him Pontoon and he's promised to show me his latest playstation game.' Darius slumped down and put his feet on the opposite settee next to Oliver. Cherry thought Oliver was about to explode.

'How about me?' Darius asked Cherry.

'How about you what?' she asked totally bemused.

'I could look after Jay, then you two can go off on your little jaunt . . . '

'It is not a little jaunt, it's business,'

Oliver said interrupting. 'And anyway, there's no way you can look after the hotel and Jay.'

Cherry was astonished. Why would one of the guests be looking after the hotel? She glanced first at one of the men and then the other.

Darius looked puzzled, then revealed, 'Oliver is my big brother. Didn't he tell you?'

7

'Just sit down and tell, will you,' pleaded Pat watching as Cherry paced up and down the small staff room.

More than anything she wanted to confide in her friend, but she knew that as soon as she'd said the words they'd become a reality. The truth was that she would have to move out of the chalet and then not only would she be homeless again, but Mrs Talbot would make sure Jay was taken away from her. As she tried to smile, Cherry felt tears forming. She burst out, 'Oh Pat, what will I do? Now I'll have to admit to living in the chalet.'

'I don't see why,' shrugged Pat, her hand hovering as ever over the biscuit tin. Cherry brushed at her face quickly, hoping Pat didn't see her. 'I told Darius I was living there — even told him to keep it quiet because the management didn't know. How embarrassing is that?'

'But Darius won't say anything,' declared Pat through a mouthful of chocolate digestive. 'He likes you and Jay and wouldn't do anything to make you unhappy. In fact,' she smiled, her eyes dancing, 'I think he may have the hots for you.'

'Rubbish — he's just a boy,' declared Cherry, momentarily sidetracked. She'd never thought of Darius like that. He was fun, he was good company, but nothing more. In some way it would be an advantage if she could have those sorts of feelings for him. Now Cherry owned up to the fact that since she'd met Oliver she wouldn't be able to think romantically about another man ever again. He'd stolen her heart and was holding it to ransom. If only he felt the same way about her everything would be perfect. If anything she seemed to irritate him.

Pat smiled before continuing. 'Anyway, let's get back to the question in hand.

Why don't you have a word with Darius to put your mind at rest? I'm sorry, Cherry, of course I can see how worrying it is. After all, there's Jay to think about as well. It is pretty serious, isn't it?'

Cherry nodded as Pat put her hand on her arm. 'You do understand why I have to tell Oliver, don't you?'

'Not really,' confessed Pat, 'but if you think it's for the best . . . '

'It's not fair for Darius to have to keep a secret like that. He'd be torn in his loyalties.' As ever, when flummoxed Cherry flapped a duster around. Now she spotted a cobweb with glee and attacked it with vigour. This was the distraction she needed.

'Do put that duster down. I can see through you, you know. You always start cleaning things when you're worried. I suppose you'll be starting on the windows next.'

'Yes,' confirmed Cherry, ducking to avoid the tea towel coming her way from her amused friend.

Pat watched Cherry for a few minutes before saying, 'You could always come and stay with us. Maurice loves seeing Jay and you know I think the world of you both.'

To Cherry it would be the answer to a prayer. Pat and Maurice were a lovely couple and she and Jay had been to their house for meals a couple of times. Maurice loved fishing and kept Jay enthralled with his own version of tales of the riverbank. A grin escaped her as she remembered Jay's look of awe as Maurice was telling him about his latest big catch. But it wouldn't be fair, Cherry decided firmly. Maurice hadn't been well and Pat already had extra work to do looking after him when she got home from the hotel.

'It's so kind of you, Pat, but it isn't a long term solution and you've got your own agenda. No, I'll just have to face it out with Oliver. You're a good friend.' She smiled, hugging Pat.

'Why not have a word with Darius? See what he has to say about it?' Pat pursed her lips and lifted an eyebrow. 'You've got Jay to think of as well, you know.'

Cherry's instincts were to be upfront and honest, but she knew what the outcome would be. Perhaps she should speak to Darius and ask him if he could keep a secret. She dusted Pat's biscuit crumbs into her hand as she thought of the possibility of being allowed to stay at the chalet. Of course Oliver wouldn't let her stay, but if he and Darius were brothers, wouldn't fifty per cent of the permission be enough? That is, if Darius agreed to it.

What choice did she have? She couldn't stay with Pat and there was nowhere else. Then again, her conscience didn't lie easy when she thought of involving Darius. He was a pleasant young man and she had no right to encourage him to be less than truthful to his brother. It wasn't right.

'Day dreaming again? Not sweet on them both, are you?' Pat laughed.

'No, of course not,' retorted Cherry,

tossing her curls.

'Just the one, then?' Pat pushed.

'You've had enough biscuits, Pat O'Brien. You'll be bursting out of your uniform before you know it.'

Pat giggled. 'All right, I'll give up asking.' Her face grew serious as she said, 'It's difficult, I know, but I don't want to see you and Jay homeless or jobless, or worse.'

What could be worse, wondered Cherry. Then the full force of her dilemma hit her. If, no, when Oliver found out about her present accommodation he'd not only sack her for being deceitful, but she'd never see him again. If it was up to her, she could easily pack her bags and sleep under a hedge somewhere, but that was impossible because of Jay. It was a circle that couldn't be squared. Cherry's instinct for flight was very strong, but she knew it would solve nothing. She had to make a plan.

'As I have to leave the chalet, I'll have nowhere to live,' she said, slowly.

'Yes, love, I know. We've been over that. You've got to live somewhere.'

'So, let's see what we've got,' said Cherry decisively. She counted off on her fingers, 'One, I confess to Oliver that Jay and I are living in one of his chalets without permission. Two, he tells me to move out. Three, I can't continue to work here as I'll have nowhere to live. Four, he sacks me as well for being dishonest. Five, I'll . . .'

'It's depressing, isn't it? So why go there?' asked Pat. She shook Cherry's arm gently. 'Honestly, Cherry, I think you should reconsider this honesty plan of yours. We keep coming back to the fact that it's not just you who's going to suffer.' Cherry knew Pat wouldn't speak like that if she wasn't anxious for her and Jay's future. Everything she lived for was at stake now.

The fact that Jay could be taken away from Cherry lay between them like an abyss. Also, Cherry couldn't quite face up to the fact that she may never see Oliver again. However, she'd always brought Jay up to be honest. It seemed that one way or another she was destined to let him down.

* * *

Having made the decision to tell Oliver the truth, Cherry still couldn't bring herself to make her way to his office. As she left the staff room she slipped on her jacket and then went out of the staff entrance to head for the river. Although the grass was still damp and sparkling from a shower, the sun was shining and the vegetation by the river was all the shades of green imaginable. The reflection of the trees in the river was almost a perfect mirror image. A drop of water from the tree she was standing under slipped behind her jacket collar and down her back making Cherry shiver. She wanted to spread her arms wide, grab the view and keep it for ever. There was something about the river which gave her the feeling that life was good and her worries were just drops in this huge expanse of water. Some ducks waddled over to her expecting bread and made her laugh with their eagerness. She felt better now and ready to face the task ahead.

Oliver's office door was firmly closed against her. Cherry tapped gently, but there was no reply. The strengthening effect of the river was wearing off. She took a few steps away thinking that maybe she should come back later, but reminded herself it wasn't fair on Darius to leave her deception a moment longer. She went back to the door and tapped again. Once again there was no answer.

'He won't hear that,' Pat said passing with a pile of table linen. Stopping, she put the pile of neatly pressed linen on a console table. 'Don't look so worried. He's a nice man, very thoughtful. I expect he'll be fine about it.' She gave Cherry a hug. 'Let me,' she said banging on the door before whispering, 'Good luck,' and carrying on with her work.

'I'm going to need it,' Cherry replied pushing open the door when she heard Oliver's abrupt, 'Come in.' Cherry's heart beat a little faster when she saw Oliver smiling at her from the other side of his desk.

'Ah, Cherry, glad you've turned up. I've just printed off some information from a website I found. I thought it might be of interest.' He waved a sheaf of papers at her. 'There's more good news too about this boat idea. I've been on to a couple of firms and got some good prices. I just need you to take a look with me. I'm sure you can manage a day trip can't you? We could take a picnic, or have a pub lunch, whatever you fancy.'

'The thing is, Oliver . . . '

'We can arrange a convenient date, the sooner the better. And the other bit of good news is that I've persuaded Darius to go to the conference. It wasn't exactly easy and I've had to promise him a couple of weeks off later in the summer, but I did it.'

Oliver was grinning like a small boy who's just won a conker fight. 'It will be good for him to go to the conference. He'll have to get up in the morning and attend lectures and workshops. And he'll have to make sure he's dressed smartly, not just in tracksuits and trainers. It might even spark an interest and make him more enthusiastic about joining the business. He has no sense of purpose. At the moment he's just drifting along, totally financed by his doting mother.' Detecting a feeling of bitterness rising and quenching his enthusiasm for the hotel he changed tack, 'Come and take a seat, Cherry, we have a lot to discuss.'

Cherry had been thinking how lovely it would be that Oliver wasn't going away and would be in the hotel when she realised it wouldn't affect her because she wouldn't be here. She was in turmoil. How could she have been so stupid? She only had herself to blame. Now she would lose everything including Jay when that dreadful Talbot woman found out they had nowhere to live. She stifled a sob. 'I haven't got much to say so I think I'll stand,' Cherry muttered twisting her hands together. 'If you don't mind, that is,' she added quickly.

Oliver was concerned. He'd been more than disappointed about the conference, but he'd consoled himself with the thought of future days away together. But looking at her now he could see that she was very worried and he wondered what the next bombshell was going to be. He'd been so wrapped up in his enthusiasm for the hotel and then his delight at persuading Darius to go to the conference, he'd completely missed the look of worry on Cherry's face.

'I've got to leave,' she said quietly.

'What?' He hadn't expected anything as dramatic as this. He stood up and paced to the window. Perhaps she was reconciled with Jay's father. Was it possible in such a short space of time? 'Why?' he added barely able to speak.

'I haven't been honest with you.'

He turned to see Cherry gazing at him with her clear blue eyes. Now he was sure, it was something to do with her ex. She'd been hiding something about their relationship. But there hadn't been any reason for her to tell him the truth about her relationship with Jay's father. 'I see,' was all he could think of to say.

'I don't think you do see, Oliver. I've taken advantage of you as my employer. I'm really sorry, I shouldn't have done it.'

He couldn't help but smile wishing that she'd taken advantage of him as a man too. He longed to take her in his arms and kiss away all her cares, but it sounded as though someone else was about to do that.

'You won't find it so amusing when I tell you what I've done.' Cherry picked at some imaginary fluff on her sleeve.

'Go on and for goodness sake sit down, you're making me nervous.' He sat back at his desk in an effort to make her do likewise.

Cherry sat nervously on the edge of the hard-backed chair opposite where he was. She was chewing on her lip and he could just barely resist rushing over to her and telling her everything was going to be all right, just so long as she forgot all about Jay's dad and concentrated on the hotel. And, of course, him.

'It's just that . . . the thing is . . . Jay and I are living in one of the chalets. I didn't get your permission. We just moved in.'

'Is that it?' Relief surged through his body and his eyes began to twinkle once again.

'No. We're not paying rent. We just moved in when the boat sank. We didn't have anywhere else to go. We were homeless. I was desperate. I thought they'd take Jay away. I couldn't bear to lose him. It was nothing to do with Pat . . . or anyone else.'

'Come on now, we all know good

hearted Pat. It was her idea, right?' He knew how kind Pat was. He'd been at the receiving end of her kindness many a time especially when he'd been younger. He'd often found surprise food parcels in his trunk when he'd unpacked at boarding school. He'd always known it was Pat and not his mother who'd been so thoughtful.

'Please, don't blame her. She really can't afford to lose her job,' Cherry pleaded sincerely.

'I know how to deal with Pat.'

Tears rolled down Cherry's cheeks and Oliver pulled a tissue from the box on his desk and passed it to her. 'I'll send for her now.' He reached for his phone and called reception to find Pat and send her in. So much for Pat's promise that he'd be fine about the chalet and that he was thoughtful.

Her friend entered the room without knocking and said a cheery, 'Hello, Oliver, can I help?'

Cherry wrung her hands. 'I'm sorry, Pat, I said it wasn't your fault.'

'I guess you put her in one of the chalets that needs renovating.'

Pat nodded. 'It was no loss to the hotel's profits except the cost of a little electricity. I was sure you wouldn't mind.'

'No, I don't mind because you were looking after the welfare of a member of staff. It was a typical gesture. In fact, Pat, I've been considering a pay rise for you for some time. You're proving to be one of my most valuable members of staff. Well, you were Mother's too. You're on the next step of the pay scale as of the beginning of next month, but I'll make sure there's a bit of a bonus on your next pay slip too.'

Pat's face lit up. 'That's fantastic. I'll be able to save a bit and take Maurice away for a few days. We haven't been anywhere for ages. We could visit some of our old haunts at Hunstanton. We used to go there regularly when we were younger. It will do him so much good. He hasn't been right since the op and the treatment gets him down.

Thank you so much, Oliver.' Pat walked round the desk and gave him a peck on the cheek, 'Your mum would be so proud of you.'

'She often told me how the hotel would fall apart without you, Pat, and that she was never going to let you retire.'

'Well, we'll see about that. I don't intend carrying on for ever. Not even for you. Is there anything else before I go?'

'If you're thinking of going to Hunstanton, I could give you the name of a hotel. A friend of mine runs it, she'll give you good rates if you mention me.'

Pat grinned widely again. 'I'd forgotten Rebecca's living there now. Your old flame.'

'Yes,' Oliver looked abashed. 'I know Mother kept you informed with all the ups and downs of our relationship.'

Cherry, who was enormously relieved that Pat was being given a pay rise and not the sack, was beginning to feel like a spare part. But she was intrigued by the conversation. One thing that amazed her was the easy familiarity between employer and employee. But she was surprised at the strength of her feeling of jealousy as they talked of Rebecca, obviously a serious girlfriend of Oliver's.

'In fact when you've set a date, how about I run you and Maurice down there? I could catch up with Rebecca over lunch. It will be great to see her again. I'm looking forward to it already. Good, sorted.' Oliver looked pleased with the arrangements.

Cherry felt like bursting into tears. Nothing was going right for her. Ever since the boat had flooded she'd made a mess of things. Now Pat was looking at her with a worried expression.

'Oliver's friend, Rebecca, has just had twin girls. Oliver was best man at the wedding. No doubt he'll be a godfather too.' As Pat left the room after kindly explaining the situation, Cherry resolved to take a firm grip of herself. She really must get a hold on things; her feelings for Oliver, keeping a job and finding somewhere permanent for Jay and her to live. She wanted more than anything to keep Jay and give him some security and she was determined to concentrate on that and not her feelings for this man who was now glaring at her. His face had set hard.

'There's nothing for it. You'll have to move immediately.'

Cherry's face crumpled. She couldn't believe this was the same man who'd just shown such consideration to Pat. Nor could she believe that she was such a bad judge of character. She fled from the room tears streaming down her face.

8

I can't believe he shouted at you,' whispered Pat. She looked across her sitting room to where Maurice and Jay were doing a jigsaw puzzle at the table. They were so engrossed, Cherry doubted that they could hear what was being said, but all the same she was pleased that Pat was keeping her voice low.

Cherry couldn't believe that Oliver had shouted at her either, but he had. If someone had told her he had a nasty side to him she wouldn't have believed them. For a second she wished she hadn't been honest, but then she looked at Jay and knew that she had done the right thing in setting him a good example. Besides to him it was a good solution even if he didn't realise all the implications.

It had been an adventure to live in

the chalet and have a bedroom to himself and play games with Darius. Now it was still an adventure to be staying with his mother in Pat's spare bedroom doing jigsaws with Maurice and being fed delicious things by Pat. Cherry sighed deeply.

'Thank you so much, Pat. I know you offered us a roof over our heads before, but we really are in need now.' She sat forward in her chair, looking around the room. 'You've got a lovely home. It's so cosy and inviting. I hope I can find somewhere quickly. We don't want to be a nuisance.'

'You're welcome to stay as long as you like,' replied Pat. 'Just look at Maurice. I haven't seen him so contented for a long time.' The two women looked over at Maurice who, absorbed as he was in his jigsaw puzzle, had a smile playing at his lips. From time to time he nudged Jay and held out a cardboard piece. Jay would frown and then point excitedly at a space. At this rate, all the jigsaws would be done.

Cherry resolved to buy some more from the charity shop next time she went to town. Or perhaps she could borrow some from the hotel. She pulled herself up sharply as she remembered that she didn't work there any more. She also remembered that she had to steal back there and get the rest of their belongings. Now that was going to be a very difficult mission.

Meanwhile, back at the hotel, Oliver had marched around the grounds trying to make sense of the last couple of hours. He'd been to the chalet where he'd hoped to find Cherry and knocked at the door. There was no reply. He didn't like to peer through the windows, but she had to be there. As she'd said, she had nowhere else to go. Then it struck him. Of course, Pat would offer her and Jay a room.

He strode off to his office intent on ringing Pat. As soon as he punched in the numbers, he knew he couldn't phone Pat. What would he say to her? It would seem as if he were checking up

88

on Cherry and it would intrude on Pat's privacy. Since taking over the hotel, Oliver had made a decision to draw a line between work and home with his employees. That way they would know that when they were home, they could switch off and enjoy their leisure time. His intention was to make the lives of the staff as easy as he could. That was why he couldn't understand what he'd done or said to make Cherry storm off like that. He looked across at the desk which he'd hoped she'd occupy. It was uncosily tidy. He remembered how alive the office had seemed when she'd sat there. As he inhaled deeply, he caught the remnants of her perfume and looked around quickly half expecting to see her smiling at him, assuring him that she'd made a mistake and she wanted to put the clock back to when everything was all right between them. But the room was empty.

Unable to settle in the oppressive office, Oliver made his way out of the front of the hotel, pausing only to take an umbrella from the stand just inside the door. The fine rain freshened everything except him. Automatically he headed around the side of the hotel to the river. It reminded him of Cherry. He often wondered about her life on the narrow boat, imagining her and Jay sitting together in the evenings reading or chatting. It must be wonderful to have such a close relationship. A sudden constriction in his throat made him realise that he missed his mother. How he wished she'd been there for him when he was a boy. Increasing his pace he scolded himself for harbouring grudges from so long ago.

It was getting dark now and the moon cast its light across the river. How beautiful everything looked. Oliver was surprised at himself for noticing. Normally he was indifferent to such romantic notions. Grunting to himself, he continued his walk which he knew would take him past Cherry's chalet once again. He resolved that he'd only knock if there was a light on. After all, he had to consider Jay who may be in bed by now.

Scarcely aware that he was holding his breath, Oliver exhaled noisily when a light showed at the front window of the chalet. Marching to the door, he rapped hard and pulled down the umbrella.

★   ★   ★

Cherry was startled when the knock came at the door. Pat had lent her a large suitcase on wheels which she had very nearly filled with Jay's things. Now she was starting on her own belongings. She had to put a light on, but had hoped that no one would be about to see it. Who could be at the door? As she wondered this, she instinctively knew that it would be Oliver. Probably checking up on her to make sure she'd gone. She poked her head around the sitting room door and saw his familiar outline through the glass front door.

Catching her breath, she knew she was trapped. He could tell she was there; the light was on. It would be rude to ignore him. She decided that she'd ask him in out of the rain and make sure he knew she was packing. She'd be out of his hair very quickly.

'Hello Oliver. Come in.' Cherry stood back to allow him to enter the chalet. However, he didn't move.

'Where on earth have you been?' he shouted. 'I've been looking everywhere for you.'

Cherry wondered if all their conversations from now on would be shouting contests until she remembered that this was probably the last time she'd ever see him.

'We're living with Pat. I just came to get the last of our things. See.' She indicated the full case and empty cupboards. 'It won't take me long to pack these last few things and then I'll be out of your way.' Cherry felt her chin wobbling and ducked her head so Oliver wouldn't see.

But Oliver was intent on walking through the chalet. Cherry suddenly felt furious with him. 'There's no need to check up on up me,' she snapped. 'I know it was wrong of me to live here without telling you, I've apologised and now I'm packing. What more can I do?'

'The chalet's in an appalling condition,' he fumed.

Cherry felt she'd been slapped in the face. One thing she'd been very careful about was keeping the place clean. 'I'll scrub it again before I leave.' Now she couldn't wait to go. It would be a relief to get away from this man, this chalet and everything.

Oliver stood in front of her. 'Cherry, I didn't mean . . . The chalet's beautifully clean,' he said softly. Gently putting his hands on her shoulders, he said, 'There seems to be a misunderstanding. When I said that you'll have to move, I meant that this place is far too ramshackle for you and Jay. Look at it,' he said. Together they let their eyes flicker over the chalet. Oliver saw a less than well maintained property; Cherry saw her home. 'My plan was that you and Jay should move to one of the pretty cottages nearer the river. These places are more than ready for renovation.'

Cherry gasped. 'But you shouted at me,' she said biting back a grin as she realised she sounded like a sulky child.

'I didn't mean to be unkind. Forgive me?' Oliver looked down at her desperately waiting for her answer.

'I'm not sure.' She was teasing him now. 'What are the cottages like?'

'Come with me and I'll show you,' urged Oliver, relief washing over him as he heard the mocking tone in her voice. His world was back the right way round now and he wanted to make sure it stayed that way. He'd never met anyone as sensitive yet strong-willed as Cherry and he knew he was falling in love with her.

'This is so pretty,' enthused Cherry. She'd forgotten that she'd ever been cross with Oliver. Now that he'd explained, everything made sense. The cottage really was lovely. There were two bedrooms, a kitchen cum living room and a little bit at the front where they could sit and look at the river. It was perfect. There was only one problem now. 'How much is the rent?' she asked, crossing her fingers and hoping she'd be able to afford it.

Oliver puckered his lips and frowned. 'Well they are quite expensive of course with their prime river location and superior furnishings. However, there is a staff discount and you'll be offered a generous expense account now that you're my adviser.'

Cherry opened her mouth to object to this obvious charitable gesture, then closed it again as she realised she wasn't in a position to haggle. 'So what will the rent be?' she repeated.

Oliver muttered to himself, putting his head comically on one side as though working out some great arithmetical challenge. 'From what I can tell, you and Jay will live here free and have your meals at the hotel. They'll be included as part of your salary, of course.'

Cherry couldn't contain herself any longer. She put her arms around Oliver and hugged him tightly. 'Pat said you were a lovely man,' she breathed softly.

'And what do you say?' asked Oliver. 'I say she's right.' So close to him, Cherry sank her face into his damp jacket and felt that if the world ended now, she'd be happy.

After what seemed like an age, Oliver gently disengaged himself. 'I'll help you move your things. Come on.' He took her by the hand and led her back to the chalet.

Used to being independent, Cherry had to stop herself from saying that she could manage on her own. She could, but she didn't want to. For once she forgot about Jay and surrendered herself to some time with Oliver.

9

With mixed feelings, Cherry was hesitant about going into work after the weekend. She wanted to see Oliver, but didn't know if he would ignore her, perhaps regretting their physical contact. Usually she felt quite cheerful when she was preparing for work. She changed into her overalls and tied her hair back in a ponytail without saying a word to Pat.

'Are you all right?' Pat asked as she watched Cherry stuff her clothes into her locker.

'Fine,' she replied plastering a false smile on her face. 'Must get on.'

It wasn't like Cherry not to want to chat and Pat was worried about her friend. She would have expected her to be singing now that she had somewhere to live and was reconciled with Oliver. She'd had so many set backs it was no wonder she'd been down, but surely she should be happy now. Pat resolved to keep more of an eye on her and Jay.

Cherry felt embarrassed when she bumped into Oliver as she was making her way up the stairs to the first floor. She could still feel the roughness of his damp jacket on her cheek.

'Let me,' Oliver said taking from her the box of cleaning materials she was carrying.

'I'm sure you have better things to do with your time,' she said as she unlocked the door of the first room she had to clean.

'Probably, but I'd rather be here chatting to you. You'll be pleased to know Darius set off for the conference this morning. No more gambling for Jay for a while. That brother of mine is a bad influence. Anyway, he seemed quite cheerful about going today. He seems to think there are going to be some attractive young women there. That's all he seems to have on his mind . . . ' He tailed off, embarrassed, and sat on a chair by the window watching Cherry as she stripped the bed. Feeling his eyes on her, Cherry stopped what she was doing and turned to face him.

'Oliver,' she said feeling her face flush, 'we mustn't get close again. I'm your employee. We've got to work together and I've got Jay to think of.' Looking at him now she wanted to relive the moments when she'd hugged him and he'd taken her hand.

'Mmm, you're probably right,' Oliver said gazing out of the window.

Cherry was disappointed. He might have protested, made her feel that it had meant at least something to him. She turned and bashed the pillows into shape.

'But as you say we do have to work together and . . . as your employer of course . . . I'd like you to go with me to look at the boats I was telling you about. I think we should make the decision together. Whether we like them and how many to buy. I'd like to go tomorrow if that fits in with your arrangements.'

'Tomorrow? I can't. I'm so sorry, but as you know it's the school holiday and I can't leave Jay all day to fend for himself. But then I could bring him. That would solve the problem. Would that be okay?'

'Will he be safe in a boat?' Oliver asked hopefully.

Cherry laughed. 'That's a joke, right?' But Oliver wasn't laughing. 'You don't want him to come, do you? We've just spent the last few years living on a boat. If Jay doesn't know about the danger of water then I really don't know who does.'

'All right then,' Oliver huffed, 'as long as we don't have to eat fast food for lunch.'

'He only eats burgers when we're out,' Cherry teased.

Oliver groaned. 'I'm not very good with children. I'm never quite sure what to say to them. Do you speak to them in simple language or treat them like you would an adult?'

'Just be yourself, Oliver. I'm sure you'll get on with Jay. He always gets on with everyone.'

'Thanks very much,' Oliver said huffily. 'You know Darius is the sociable one. He gets on with everyone too, all ages from babies to ninety year olds. Couldn't Pat . . .'

'No, she couldn't. I'm not taking advantage of her.' Cherry was quick to dismiss that idea.

But after Oliver had left the room she longed to rush off and find Pat to ask if she'd care for Jay. The thought of spending a day alone with Oliver was thrilling, but then she remembered what she'd just said to Oliver about being his employee. There would be no more holding hands with him. Although she'd thought she'd never fall in love again after Alan had left, she was beginning to understand what falling in love was really like. She'd never felt quite like this before.

★　★　★

Oliver waited in the hotel foyer. He'd decided to dress casually in jeans and a shirt. In spite of her remoteness his mother would have insisted he took a change of clothes as he invariably fell in when he was boating. He remembered punting in Cambridge with friends as a teenager, getting the pole stuck in the mud and holding on a little too long until he fell in. And it was just his luck that it had been where the place was thick with tourists. He didn't want to make a fool of himself in front of Cherry or Jay. He could do with Jay's support.

'Hi!' Cherry took him by surprise. He jumped up from his chair.

'Hello,' he said taking her hands and admiring her slim figure and pretty blouse. He peered behind her as she pulled her hands from his. 'Where's Jay?' he asked.

'Maurice wanted to take him fishing and reluctantly I agreed.' Cherry pulled her hands out of his grasp and crossed her fingers behind her back. She'd called to see Pat and Maurice the previous evening and asked if Jay could spend the day with Maurice. Pat in particular had been very enthusiastic about the plan. Maurice and Jay were now down on the river with their fishing rods and would happily spend the whole day there. Cherry had made thick sandwiches along with two large thermos flasks of tea. She'd promised to pick up fish and chips on the way home although Maurice had joked with Jay that she needn't bother as they'd be catching their own supper.

Cherry was happy rowing the boat, with Oliver lying back on the cushions clutching a glass of wine.

'This is the life, cheers,' he said raising his glass.

'I think we'll pull into the bank in the shade of those trees and then we'll be able to enjoy the lunch you've brought.' When Cherry had brought the boat alongside and secured it to the trunk of a tree she hopped back on the boat and settled on the cushion Oliver had thrown her. He then passed her some pitta bread filled with minted falafel and salad and arranged chicken wraps and fruit on a plate, before handing her a glass of wine.

'To boating,' Oliver raised his glass.

Cherry raised hers too, but felt sad at the thought of her old home being bought and repaired by some stranger. 'I suppose things change,' she murmured aloud.

'They certainly do,' Oliver agreed. It wasn't so long ago he'd been besotted by Rebecca and now he barely gave her a thought. All his thoughts were now of this lively young woman who looked so grave right now. Then there was the hotel.

'What is it, Oliver?' Cherry asked on seeing his thoughtful face.

'Just thinking how quickly things do change. I was working in the City when my mother died leaving me the hotel. It was only four months ago. I didn't know what to do at first. I had a good life there and enjoyed my job. Lots of friends, a good social life. It was difficult to make a decision, but I thought if I didn't come and try to make a go of the hotel I'd regret it for the rest of my life.'

Cherry reached for a wrap. 'Any regrets about coming here?'

'None at all,' he said solemnly as he gazed at her.

'I'm sorry about your mother,' Cherry said looking away and hoping by changing the subject she'd say nothing she'd regret. Sitting on the gently rocking boat with Oliver just an arm's reach away was almost more than she could bear. 'I can't really say I ever got to know her, she was quite distant with her employees.'

'We weren't close. She was a rather distant mother too, but I do miss her.' There was a catch in his voice.

Cherry reached forward and took his hand. She squeezed it gently and was going to pull her hand away when Oliver grasped it firmly. She'd definitely made the right decision leaving Jay behind. Oliver pulled her towards him and gently kissed her. She felt an overwhelming wave of desire as he gazed into her eyes.

'Cherry, I just want to say . . . '

But the moment was lost as Cherry leapt up, almost overturning the boat. 'Look we've drifted from the bank,' she shouted, 'and I've left the oars there.'

'Sit down, Cherry, you're making me sea sick.' Oliver grinned at the ridiculousness of their situation.

Cherry sat back down, red-faced. 'You'll think me such a fool, not keeping the oars in the boat. We should have brought Jay, he's got more sense than me.' Hearing Oliver laugh she too saw the funny side of their situation and pulling the cushion out from behind her, threw it at Oliver almost knocking him off balance.

'I promise I won't hold this against you as long as you're prepared to do the swimming.'

Cherry tested the water with her hand. 'Way too cold for me. Anyway, it's your outing. I'm prepared to meet you halfway, I'll apologise for not being much good at tying ropes to trees.'

Oliver hadn't enjoyed himself so much for months and was quite happy to dive into the water. All that troubled him was the question of how much clothing to keep dry. He slipped his shirt off, but decided he'd have to endure wet jeans for the rest of the day. Jumping in he rocked the boat and could hear Cherry squealing then clapping and shouting encouragement. Bobbing up he pulled the boat back to the bank. Once on dry land he secured the boat and watched as Cherry leapt out clutching his shirt.

'Here we are, Oliver, slip this back on,' she said holding the shirt out for him. She couldn't fail to notice his toned, masculine body. Being with him was becoming more and more difficult especially as she'd told herself she must regard him as her employer and nothing more. Oliver was shivering and reached out for her.

'Warm me up, Cherry, that water's freezing.'

It took all Cherry's willpower to resist. She turned and stepped back to the boat. 'Come on, Oliver, let's get back in so that I can row us back to the yard. Then we can drive home with the heating on. It might be sunny, but it's a cold day for May and we don't want you going down with anything.'

'This always happens to me,' Oliver said miserably, his good mood slowly dripping away. 'I'm always the one who gets wet.'

Oliver didn't say much on the drive back to the hotel and Cherry didn't know whether to chat or keep quiet. As they drove into the staff car park Oliver slammed on the brakes. 'Have you seen that?' he said angrily.

Cherry couldn't see anything unusual.

'That car!'

It was a red TVR and meant nothing to Cherry.

'It belongs to Darius. What the hell's he doing back so soon?'

Oliver was polite enough to open the car door for Cherry before marching off to find out what Darius was up to. Cherry couldn't see a problem. She'd been surprised when Darius had gone to the conference, but he wasn't the sort of man, in Cherry's opinion, to spend a few days being told what to do. Obviously, he didn't have an overwhelming interest in the hotel business. Hopefully Oliver would have time to change out of his squelching jeans before berating Darius.

She opened the car boot and started unloading the picnic things. It had been a wonderful time and she'd so enjoyed being on the river. Crumpled up on the floor of the boot were Oliver's socks. He said he couldn't drive without shoes and his feet were so uncomfortable with wet socks. It was funny, reflected Cherry, a giggle threatening, how the most unlikely men could have sexy feet. Tucking the still damp socks into her pocket, she carried the picnic things back into the hotel. Having sorted them all out in the staff room, she headed for the cottage.

Cherry was delighted to have all these rooms to herself. Having separate bedrooms and more living space was wonderful. She'd stayed up late the night before trying out the oven. And it was such a luxury to have a washing machine and loads of hot water on tap. Almost without thinking, she ran herself a deep bath, pouring in vanilla and cocoa butter scented crème. Then she dashed to the bedroom for a book and portable radio. If her day on the river was cut short, she'd make up for it by spending some time in the bath! A luxury she'd been without while living on the boat.

Very comfortable and warm, Cherry turned the pages of her book soothed by the piano music playing in the background. Suddenly, she sat upright splashing water over the side of the bath. What on earth was she doing?

Technically, she was still supposed to be at work. Because of her time on the river and the picnic, she'd forgotten that it was a working day out. Oliver had said he needed to know what sort of boats they wanted and how many.

Pulling out the plug, she scrambled out of the bath, drenching her book, and dried herself before dressing in cream trousers and a lilac blouse. Her hair had gone frizzy from the dampness in the bathroom, but she had no time to try and tame it, just wield a brush through it.

Ten minutes later she was sitting at the desk in the office, a pad of paper in front of her chewing on the end of a biro.

'Ah good, you've made a start.' Oliver came into the room looking smart in a suit again, giving no indication that he'd stormed off, fallen in the river or kissed her so deliciously.

Cherry pretended to be engrossed with scribbling lists onto the page and didn't look up. Eventually, she handed over the pad and said, 'Here are my ideas. I hope you'll find them satisfactory. Now, if it's all right with you,' she glanced at her watch, 'I have to go and pick up Jay.'

Oliver's head jerked up. 'But I thought he was with Maurice.'

'He's spent the day with him, yes, but I can't expect him to look after Jay any longer. I think I've done all I can today. If I think of anything further, I'll make notes this evening and continue tomorrow. Now, if you'll excuse me.'

'Cherry . . . ,' Oliver started, but she'd swept from the room leaving only a fragrance of vanilla behind her.

* * *

'It was great, Mum. You should have been there. I caught a whopper!' Jay exclaimed. 'It was that big.' He extended his arms as far as he could.

'I'm sorry I couldn't bring fish and chips. We came home earlier than we expected and The Flying Cod wasn't open then,' said Cherry. 'We could have cooked your fish.'

'Oh, most fishermen throw their catch back. It's the thrill of the catch, not the kill,' Jay recited.

Cherry smiled to herself. Jay and Maurice had evidently had a good chat.

'What shall we do now, Mum?' They were lounging on the settee in the cottage watching the news on TV, but Jay was too restless to settle.

'Come on then. I'll buy you an ice cream at the hotel and you can eat it in the lounge.'

Eagerly, Jay scrambled to his feet and was out the door before Cherry could switch off the TV and grab her purse.

'Darius! I thought you were away. Look Mum, it's Darius.'

'The conference didn't take your interest then?' enquired Cherry feeling a bit uncomfortable.

'It was quite boring, Cherry. I thought I'd have more fun playing Pontoon with my mate here, so I came back.' He took a pack of cards from his

113

pocket, cut them, shuffled them elaborately and slapped them down on the table. 'Ready when you are.'

'Do you still want that ice cream?' asked Cherry.

'I'd rather play cards first. Can I, Mum?'

Cherry left them to it and sank into a deep armchair by the window. Exhausted by all the goings on of the last couple of days, Cherry closed her eyes and tried to relax. Things were going well, she told herself. Jay had had a good day out and was now having a happy time. They had somewhere great to live and she didn't need to impose on Pat and Maurice. She promised herself an early night. Hopefully, she wouldn't be overwhelmed by bad dreams of Oliver. Behind closed eyelids, she thought of what might have happened if she hadn't left the blasted oars on the bank. She remembered Oliver's face with his inviting lips nearing hers. Not being able to think of what might have been, she snapped her eyes open. Then wished she hadn't.

'Mrs Talbot? What are you doing here?' Cherry struggled out of her reverie and looked up at her worst nightmare.

'As a matter of fact, I called in for a pot of tea on my way home. I didn't know you'd be here, I thought you'd be out with Jay especially as it's his half-term holiday.'

Cherry stood up and faced Mrs Talbot. 'Yes, he's . . . '

But Mrs Talbot didn't let her finish. 'By the look of things, it's just as well I did call in.' Her lips compressed and she looked pointedly in the direction of Jay and Darius.

'Twist,' yelled Jay, while Cherry's insides twisted.

'Oh no,' she breathed.

Just at that moment, Oliver came out of the office and passed through the lounge. Taking in the situation, he advanced on Cherry and Mrs Talbot. 'How do you do? Are you a friend of Cherry?' He beamed his most winning smile at her and extended his hand.

Short of being rude, Mrs Talbot had to shake hands with him. Cherry, not sure what was going on, but glad of the diversion, introduced her son's social worker to her boss and explained that Mrs Talbot had just popped in for a pot of tea.

'But now I find that the young boy is gambling,' she exclaimed, nodding towards the corner banquette.

Oliver's rumble of laughter took them both by surprise. 'Gambling? Oh no, Mrs Talbot. I think you've got the wrong end of the stick there. Just a minute.' He darted over to Darius, spoke briefly to him and then returned. 'The man with Jay is my brother. It's as I thought. Darius is giving Jay some homework. You know, practising adding up, that sort of thing. We used to do it with our parents during the school holidays,' he continued smoothly. 'Much better if you can make a game out of these things, I'm sure you agree, Mrs Talbot.'

Taking up the theme, Cherry said,

'Jay does need some help with his arithmetic and Darius was kind enough to volunteer. They play for matches, you know.' She was so relieved she hadn't given in and let Jay play with pennies. She stole a look at Mrs Talbot who looked uncertain.

'Good, now that's settled, would you excuse me?' Oliver took Mrs Talbot's hand once again. 'I hope we'll have the pleasure of seeing you here again soon.' He carried on through the hotel lounge before disappearing into the kitchen.

Cherry frowned at Oliver's strange behaviour, but he'd certainly saved their bacon this time and she sent silent thanks to him. 'May I get you that pot of tea, Mrs Talbot,' Cherry asked. She just wanted the woman to go, but didn't want to be seen to be hurrying her out in case she changed her mind about being satisfied with Oliver's explanation.

As Mrs Talbot and Cherry settled down at the table by the window once again, one of the waitresses appeared beside them and deposited a laden tray in front of them.

'What's this?' gasped Mrs Talbot. 'I only wanted a cup of tea.'

'Mr Fingle's compliments, madam. He thought you both deserved a full cream tea.'

They looked at the warm scones, pots of cream and strawberry jam. 'This looks scrumptious,' said Cherry, despite feeling it was a little late to be serving up a cream tea. But she was delighted to see Mrs Talbot reaching for a plate. Cherry picked up the large teapot and poured a cup of steaming tea, handing it across the table.

'These scones are delicious. It's ages since I had a cream tea,' said Mrs Talbot. 'In fact, it's ages since I had lunch.' She took a large bite of scone, leaving a trace of cream and jam on the end of her nose. Cherry laughed and passed her a serviette. Maybe she wasn't such an awful woman after all. She must have to deal with all sorts of people and Cherry was certain that it was the child's welfare which mattered most to her.

Cherry took a deep breath. 'I'd like to thank you for keeping an eye on Jay. I know it's your job to make sure that the children are looked after properly. I'm sorry if I've been less than helpful to you in the past.'

'Believe me, Cherry, I've come across a lot worse people than you.' Well, that was a backhanded compliment if ever there was one, but Mrs Talbot didn't seem to realise her gaffe. 'As a matter of fact, I remember my own father taking me shopping in order to improve my arithmetical skills. I became very accomplished at mental arithmetic. Won a prize, you know.'

Even having moved forward with her opinion of Mrs Talbot, Cherry still had difficulty trying to picture her as a young schoolchild.

As she grinned, Mrs Talbot said, 'You know, Cherry, since you've been living here, you seem a lot happier. I never did like the idea of you both living on a boat. It didn't seem suitable somehow. And, of course, the water can be so dangerous.' A small frown clouded her face. Leaning forward, she confided, 'I had a very nasty experience in a boat once, you know.'

Cherry didn't know, and couldn't imagine. All she could think of was the wonderful time she'd had in boats. First of all, living on one and then with Oliver earlier that day.

'And that little lad of yours seems very happy and settled here,' continued Mrs Talbot. She took another giant bite of scone and settled back in her chair.

Cherry looked over at Darius and Jay. Her mouth fell open as she saw Oliver sitting on the edge of the table chatting and laughing with them. Considering how annoyed he'd been with his brother not long before, Cherry could only suppose that Oliver was putting on a show for Mrs Talbot. Oliver caught her look and gave a thumbs up, along with a brilliant smile. Cherry's heart soared.

10

Oliver was enjoying sitting in the office with Cherry after all the ups and downs of the previous day. It was a sunny afternoon and beams of sunshine caught the motes of dust dancing in the air. He was still very angry with Darius and his attitude to the hotel and the conference, but felt good about his interception with Mrs Talbot and the happy outcome. Cherry had an extra spring in her step. He was hoping her good mood would include him. He wondered if he should invite her for dinner that evening. They could go to a quiet restaurant in town and get to know each other better. Although he already felt as though he knew her as well as himself, it was time they spent some proper time together.

Cherry was reading through her notes. 'So I ordered the boats this morning, the fishing rights are being dealt with by your solicitor and I'm taking delivery of ten bicycles tomorrow morning. The renovation of the old chalets is starting next week and the planning application has gone in for those pine cabins we're going to build in the wood. The builder wants to start on the roadway in July as he's sure we'll get permission for the cabins. Oh, yes, and the contractor is going to start work improving the bank for the moorings for visiting boats. I think that's everything for now, but we must think about the brochure for next year. We need to start sending them out soon. I thought we'd take some photos of the river, try and catch its mood at different times of the day. Then in the coming year we can catch the seasons ready for the next year's brochure. We need pictures of people fishing, boating and cycling.'

As she talked he watched her hair bobbing round her face and the way she frowned a little when she was thinking.

He wanted to smooth away the frown lines with his fingers and kiss her lips to take her mind away from the hotel and back to him.

'Oliver!'

'Sorry, I . . .'

'You weren't listening to a word I said. I just asked you a question. If you're not going to take any notice of me I might as well give up.' She flung her notepad on the desk.

'I'm sorry, I was preoccupied. I was thinking. Isn't it good about Mrs Talbot and how she seems to be off your back at last?'

'Mmm, all down to your cream tea. If I'd known the way to her heart was through food I'd have tried it months ago. All I had to do was offer her a ginger nut and she'd have left Jay and me alone.' Cherry giggled. 'I can't thank you enough. It's such a relief to know I can keep Jay. If I can ever help you out . . .'

'There is one thing.' Oliver made his way round the desk and, taking her hand, he knelt down beside her. He was in the classic position for a proposal, but Cherry knew that wasn't what he was about to ask. Perhaps he was going to ask her for a date. She wanted to hug him, tell him how she felt about him ... The door burst open and Darius came crashing in.

'Ah, there you are, Oliver, I've been looking everywhere for you.'

'Ever heard of knocking?' Oliver asked crossly as he stood and straightened his tie. 'Well? What do you want?' He wandered back to his chair opposite Cherry and sat down.

'A drink would be a good start.' Darius poured himself a glass of whisky from the decanter which stood on a cabinet near the window. 'Drink anyone?'

'I think I'd better go. Leave you two alone.' Cherry didn't want to be involved in whatever was going to happen between the two brothers. She couldn't imagine what Darius had barged in for and she'd never seen him drink in the afternoon before. She guessed he needed Dutch courage for some reason.

'No,' Oliver said brusquely, 'you stay here. It's your office too. I'm not having you turned out because my little brother's got himself into yet another mess. It will be money or woman trouble. What is it Darius? Go on. We've work to do. We were working when you came in.'

'If that's what you call work I'll give it a go.' Darius winked at Cherry who couldn't help but smile back.

'Everything's such a joke to you isn't it? Do you think I got where I am today by lying in bed all morning and playing for the rest of the day.'

Darius smiled wryly as he replied. 'No, you got where you are today through your inheritance.'

Oliver looked as though he'd been slapped in the face.

Darius continued, but was speaking to Cherry. 'Our father made sure Oliver's mother was all right by letting her have the hotel as part of their divorce settlement. I can see that was fair enough. But then, as Oliver well knows, the rest of Dad's empire crumbled. It wasn't a good time for him and when he died Mum and I were left with practically nothing.'

Oliver looked shamefaced. 'I'm sorry, Darius, it's just that you don't seem to be making an effort. I want to help. I've given you a chance to work with me here, but you're hardly accepting the challenge.'

Oliver didn't know what else to say. Although Darius's cavalier attitude annoyed him nevertheless he still felt affection for the younger man.

'That's because I want to do something for myself, not be given handouts by my big brother. You must be able to see that. You wouldn't want that either, we're similar to each other in some ways although you're always telling me how different we are. I haven't yet found my niche, but there's more to me than you think. I do want to make something of myself. I have ambition too.' Darius gulped at his drink. 'In fact, that's why I'm here, I've got something to tell you.'

Oliver wished more than anything that there were no more surprises and that things would settle down so that he could spend some quiet time with Cherry. He felt as though he was ageing visibly. He was sure to have grey hair soon with all the worrying he'd been doing about those he loved. He was startled to think that he'd included Cherry in that group. Had he really fallen in love? He looked across at her to see an expression of concern worrying her face. But her eyes were on Darius, not him. He felt a sudden stab of jealousy.

'Don't think I'm not grateful, but I'm going off to Spain with Seb tomorrow.' Darius raised his glass and took another gulp of the fiery liquid.

'Seb? Who the hell's Seb?' Oliver could barely speak.

'I've told you about him before, he's

an old school friend. We've kept in touch. He's into property development. He's got this real money making business going and wants me to have part of the action. He's building apartments on the Costa del Sol, but they're for the top end of the market. I'm going to be marketing executive so I'll get trips back here although we hope to sell to the expats already living there.' Darius was now sprawled in a chair cradling the glass which he'd just refilled.

'How long have you known about this?' Oliver's voice was cracking and Cherry couldn't judge if it was through disappointment or anger.

'He rang this morning . . .'

Oliver practically exploded. 'You've only just been told about this so called money making scheme and you've decided to go, just like that. It took me weeks to make the decision to come here and run the hotel and it takes you seconds to leave a good job and go haring off because of some crazy scheme.'

'We're different in that way. The thing is I don't want to work here in the hotel, I'm not ready to stagnate in this dump. It's a great life style out there for a young person, sea, sun . . . hmmm . . . what else begins with s?' He winked at Cherry again.

'Is it funny, Cherry?' Oliver asked crossly.

'No, but Darius is. I disagree with him about this place being a dump, I think it's idyllic here by the river and I wouldn't want to be anywhere else, but as Darius says we are all different. The thing is, Oliver, he's got to do things for himself, not be given handouts by you. Don't you see that he has to make his own way, even if some of the things he does are mistakes.'

'Thanks, Cherry, I might have known you'd understand. You could come too, bring Jay, we could live in a hut on the beach. I can see you barefoot in the sand.'

Cherry could tell Darius was enjoying annoying the hell out of Oliver when he grinned at her.

Oliver knew his brother was joking, but felt a pang of jealousy at the easy way Cherry and Darius were with each other. He wished he wasn't quite so stiff and formal at times like this. He knew it all went back to his unemotional childhood and being told by his mother he'd just have to get on with things when his father had left. He'd been heartbroken at the loss of his father, but he'd hidden his feelings just as his mother had wanted. Since then he'd found it hard to show his true feelings. He wished he had that easy way with people that Darius had, and that his father had had. He tried to see things from Darius's point of view. He had to admit that he too had been having doubts and thinking of packing the whole hotel thing in until he'd met Cherry. Now he was sure his life was here . . . with her. And like her he found the setting of the hotel and the surrounding area idyllic.

'Your mind's made up, but I do think

you should do a bit of research before you pack your bags.' Oliver was being practical as usual. He wished he could be a bit more spontaneous.

'Course,' Darius said.

Here goes, he thought. 'Any chance of a short break with you? What do you say, Cherry, shall we all go to Spain for a holiday?' The idea of a holiday with Cherry and Jay made him feel light hearted. It was possible for him now to imagine the three of them as a family unit.

'Wait until I've got somewhere to live and have learnt a few Spanish card games for Jay and you'll be welcome. What do you think, Cherry?' The two men were looking at Cherry expectantly, waiting for her answer.

Cherry didn't know what to say or think. Had Oliver actually just invited her and Jay on a holiday with him or was it some sort of fact finding trip for the hotel?

'I'll have to check with Jay, but it sounds good to me. You've been very good to us, Darius. Jay will miss you.'

'I'll miss him too, you must be very proud of him. I think once Oliver gets to know Jay he'll be a good replacement. In spite of what you might think, he's been a very good brother to me.'

A holiday would be nice, thought Cherry as she manoeuvred the hoover around the hallways. If Alan hadn't been so henpecked, Jay would be on holiday with him now. She reflected what it might be like to be alone in her little cottage. Well, perhaps not totally alone. A nice candlelit dinner for two with Oliver, soft music, the river lapping the bank, the moonlight . . . Idiot, she told herself, laughing out loud. Hastily, she finished the hall carpets and then put the cleaning materials away. Her watch told her she had time for a quick break before donning her hat as chief adviser to the management. Although she'd definitely accomplished a lot in the last few days, she wasn't sure they were things that Oliver really wanted for the hotel. He hadn't been very forthcoming, just nodded and stroked his chin. Cherry fancied Oliver was a bit jealous of Darius, but she wasn't sure why. They were both good-looking, easy to get on with, popular with the staff as far as she could tell and the guests always had a word for them when they were around. Oliver, however, was a bit buttoned up. Here Cherry had to shake herself out of her daydream as she imagined herself undoing those buttons . . . Perhaps now that Darius had gone to Spain, Oliver would relax a bit more.

Darius had certainly seemed cheerful that morning when he'd knocked on the cottage door very early. Jay must have been expecting him, because he was awake and ran to let him in.

'I'll miss you, Darius,' Jay had said. 'Tell me your address and I'll write to you.' Cherry had watched as Jay carefully wrote down what Darius dictated to him. Poor Jay, another person leaving him behind.

'Now don't forget,' said Darius,

bending down to look Jay in the eye, 'your school work's just as important as pontoon. When I come back, I shall want to see your school reports.'

He waggled his eyebrows and Jay giggled. Standing up straight again, Darius held out his hand to Jay and the friends shook hands. Then Darius kissed Cherry lightly on the cheek and hurried away. The TVR roared off down the drive sounding like a dragon possessed.

After a sandwich and pot of coffee, Cherry positioned herself at the desk in the office in front of the computer. Although she could type a letter, write an email and basic things like that, she was very aware that she was a bit computer illiterate. Perhaps Oliver would send her on a course. No, she didn't really fancy going away to learn about computers. There was no likelihood of Oliver and her going to the next conference either as she'd feel awkward asking Pat's help to look after Jay. Pat and Maurice had already done so much, and Darius wasn't there.

Abandoning the notebook she'd pulled towards her, she opened a new document on the computer, called it 'Cherry's notes', and started typing in her ideas and accomplishments so far. In fact it was an impressive list, but there was still a way to go. Her thoughts turned to Jay who was in the staff room with Pat while she was having her lunch. Later he would join her in the office and sit next to her either reading or drawing. Not much of a holiday for him, poor love. That gave her an idea. She started typing in a list of amusements and diversions which they may be able to implement at the hotel for the youngsters. Quite pleased with her list, she saved it in her file and decided to let Jay help her when he came in later.

When the door opened quietly, Cherry assumed it was Jay. 'Come and sit by me, sweetheart. It'll be nice to have your company.'

'Thank you, darling, but I think I'll

sit at my own desk, if you don't mind.'

It was Oliver of course and Cherry had never been so embarrassed. He always seemed to catch her out and make her blush. 'Sorry, I thought you were Jay.' She looked at Oliver and saw a grin tugging at his mouth. Laughing, she said, 'I was so engrossed in my work I didn't look to see who it was.' Wanting desperately to change the subject, Cherry asked, 'Do you want to see the lists I've made for improvements?'

'You seem to have so many lists for improvements, Cherry, that I wonder what sort of a place this was before! Quite a boring hotel, I suppose.' He turned away as his phone rang.

After he'd replaced the handset, he said, 'Bit of a panic in the kitchens. Andre wants some help. I don't suppose . . .'

'I'd love to go. He's expecting you to inspect the kitchens, you know and he's a bit nervous.'

'But he runs everything so smoothly.

I didn't think there was a need for me to go interfering.' Oliver picked up a pencil from a pile on his desk and fiddled with it. 'You seem so good with people, Cherry. They like you and confide in you. I wish I was more like that.'

For once in her life, Cherry was speechless and fled from the office for a bit of relaxation with Andre. Why did Oliver have to be so heavy? She didn't know how to answer him.

As soon as she'd gone, Oliver could have kicked himself. He'd tried to open up to her, but had failed. He'd only caused friction. A quiet knock at the door brought him back to present. 'Come in,' he called.

Jay opened the door, walked into the room. 'Is Mum here?' he asked.

'She's just gone down to the kitchens. Shouldn't be long. Come on in.' Oliver's heart sank. He was about to suggest that Jay go and join Cherry and Andre, when he wondered why it was that he felt uncomfortable with the lad.

He was well behaved, polite and articulate; if he'd been an adult, they'd have got on well. Deciding to give it his best shot, he said, 'What do you know about computers, Jay?'

'Well, we've got them at school and some of my friends have got them at home as well. I can write a story on them and print it out, but really I prefer to use a pen and paper.'

'There are other things you can do besides work,' said Oliver, his eyes twinkling with suggestion.

★ ★ ★

'It's so nice to be down here with you again, Andre,' sighed Cherry.

'What do you make of the boss? He hasn't been down here for the inspection yet.'

'That's because you're very well organised as usual.' Cherry leant against the table, 'You're not worried, are you?'

'A bit,' confessed Andre.

'There's absolutely no need. Oliver's just very busy at the moment. He wants to improve the hotel and as the kitchens are running exceptionally well, he's leaving you to it.'

'Do you mean that?' Andre blew out his cheeks. 'Oh thank you, Cherry, I was really nervous that he was putting off giving me the sack. Perhaps I'll pluck up the courage to ask for a pay rise.'

Hurrying back upstairs, Cherry remembered that Jay was due to join her in the office. She expected to find him skulking about in the corridor waiting for her. But he wasn't there. She'd just let Oliver know she was back from the kitchens and that a PR visit from him would do Andre good and then she'd look for Jay. Pushing open the office door, she was surprised to hear Jay chuckling. He was sitting at her computer with Oliver next to him. Oliver let out a roar of laughter which he didn't try to hide when he saw Cherry.

'Oliver's showing me some funny things on the computer, Mum. And I can draw things, too. Look what I've done.'

Cherry came round behind Jay and looked at the screen. Her throat tensed as she saw what he'd drawn. In an unsteady voice, she said, 'The boat. It's our boat, Jay.'

Jay nodded. 'I'm going to print it off later. I've saved it in my file,' he said, proudly.

'I think you'd better let me sit there now, love. I've got work to do.' She didn't want Oliver getting cross with Jay. She knew he found it difficult to relate to him.

'Now just a minute,' Oliver burst out, 'we haven't finished our game.'

'Oliver's teaching me Mahjong. It's wicked, Mum. If we had a computer, I'd play it all day long.'

The two heads were pressed together. Cherry wouldn't have access to her computer for a long while yet. 'I'll get some tea.' She smiled.

When she'd left the office, Oliver sat back in his chair. He'd been pleased with how well things had gone with Jay. He remembered that Darius had said he'd make a good replacement as a friend to Jay. He also remembered that Darius had said that he'd been a very good brother to him.

Guilt flooded through him as he wondered if Darius was going to Spain to get out of his way — as if he sensed that Oliver was fed up with him. The thing was, they had different mothers and had been brought up differently. That's what made them like chalk and cheese. Looking at Jay, Oliver saw how he'd been nurtured with love and affection and an instilling of confidence. Now Oliver realised he had a chip on his shoulder and at 38, it was time to get rid of it. Whatever he felt he'd missed out on by being sent to boarding school, he had to give credit where it was due. His parents had decided that he'd have a better education if they paid for it and he'd gain independence if he were away from home.

Thinking back to something else that Darius had said, Oliver knew that he'd been right. He had got where he was today because of his inheritance. It seemed that everything about him boiled down to having money.

Watching the intense expression on Jay's face as he searched the screen for matching symbols, reminded Oliver so much of Cherry. Perhaps now he should pursue her with greater intent. But what if she turned him down? Just when they seemed to be getting on well, he'd misjudged the situation. She'd been quite off hand with him on a couple of occasions when he thought he was in a position to ask her out. All their outings so far had been business-based. He'd also been a little afraid of how Jay would react to him going out with his mother. But the lad seemed relaxed in his company and for that he was pleased.

'Look, two south winds, Jay. See if

you can beat your own record.'

Jay zapped the matches and punched the air as another record win fire-cracked on the screen.

11

It was fast approaching the end of Jay's school holiday and Cherry wanted to do something really special for him. He'd been as good as gold and hadn't appeared to mind being restricted to the hotel during the day. However, Cherry wasn't working at the weekend. She was torn between the cinema and a burger meal afterwards or going to the bowling alley and then on to the Italian restaurant next door to it.

Deciding that being cooped up in the cinema wouldn't be the better option, she settled on the bowling plan. Just the two of them would be nice. It had been an exhausting week now she came to think of it, but things hadn't worked out too badly.

Today, Jay was going to go home with Pat when she finished at lunch-time and he'd have fun with her and

Maurice until Cherry collected him at tea-time. Determined to finish her lists before the weekend, she hurried to finish the cleaning and took a tray of coffee and biscuits into the office. Oliver was having a meeting with Andre in the kitchens, so he wouldn't be there to moan if she dropped crumbs into the keyboard. Opening her file, she continued with her plans.

When she heard the office door opening, she took the precaution this time of looking up to see who it was. Oliver stood there looking so handsome and gorgeous, she had to hold on to her chair to stop herself running to him. But he came over to her and, pulling her to her feet, kissed her none too gently on the lips. Questioning this move briefly, she surrendered herself to it and made the most of it. Letting her go as quickly as he'd taken hold of her, Cherry was again in turmoil. She studied his face, but there were no clues there. As he sat at his desk and got on with his work, Cherry asked, 'What was that about, Oliver?'

'I've been to see Andre. You were right, he was anxious. When I told him I was impressed with him and his kitchens, he was so pleased. We had a chat about this and that and he's going to make some suggestions, too. That'll keep you happy with yet another list.'

'That's not what I meant, Oliver and you know it,' snapped Cherry. 'I just don't know where I am with you. One minute you're kissing me and the next you're ignoring me. I don't know whether you like me or if you're upset with me. I'm doing my best for your hotel, I've got Jay to think of and, although the cottage is fantastic, I've still got to think and plan for the future.'

As she paused for breath, Oliver came and perched on the desk, facing her. He put out a hand and stroked her cheek. 'Cherry . . . ' Just as he'd been about to unleash all his feelings for her, there was a loud knock on the office door. Oliver leapt to his feet, strode

146

over and opened it.

'Can I see you a minute, Oliver? I need to change my day off next week.' One of the waitresses stood apprehensively in the open doorway. 'I'm really sorry, but we're having problems at home.'

Sensing that it would be much better for Oliver to be left in private with Suzy, Cherry took herself and her tray of dirty crockery off to the staff room.

What would have happened if Suzy hadn't come in then? Was Oliver about to declare undying love, or tell her off for reading too much into everything? Her chaotic mind needed something to set it straight again, so she began cleaning, starting with her own cup, saucer and plate. When the staff room was as she wanted it, she realised that enough time had elapsed for her to return to the office. Not sure whether she should pretend nothing had happened, or insist that Oliver continue the conversation where he left off, she was saved the worry.

The man at reception was very familiar to her. At the same moment she saw him, he waved at her and threw his travel bag on the floor.

'Cherry,' he called. 'What a relief. I thought I'd gone to the wrong hotel. No one here seems to know who Mrs Hinton is!'

They wouldn't, thought Cherry. I'm Cherry to everyone. As she let herself be held close, she wondered what had happened to bring him here

* * *

Unseen, Oliver came in search of Cherry. Poor Suzy had a very difficult home life it seemed. Hopefully, she'd be able to sort out her current troubles and he'd told her to ask him if she needed any extra time off. If anything, Suzy's problems had reinforced in him the fact that happiness doesn't come to your door, you have to make your own efforts to seize the day. Rounding the corner to reception, Oliver quickly hid himself behind a convenient screen and peeped out. Who was that man embracing Cherry? So, Cherry wasn't interested in him romantically after all. She just saw him as an employer and, possibly, a friend. Thank goodness Suzy came in when she did or he'd have made a complete idiot of himself. How on earth could he imagine that a wonderful, adorable woman like Cherry wouldn't be snapped up? Mentally kicking himself, he waited until he could slip away unseen.

★   ★   ★

'Alan! What on earth are you doing here?' Cherry was cross that her ex-husband had just turned up out of the blue. Didn't he realise she worked here, that her job depended on her being reliable and keeping a professional profile? Pushing him away from her, she repeated, 'What are you doing here?' As far as she knew he was supposed to be in Scotland.

'I thought you'd be pleased to see me.' Alan was obviously angry. 'Honestly Cherry, you haven't changed a bit. You're never satisfied. First of all you beg me to see Jay and then you shout at me when I arrive.'

'Now just a minute.' Cherry made herself count to at least ten before taking a deep breath and saying, 'Shall we start again Alan? I'm sure Jay will be delighted to see you and that's what counts. Whatever your personal arrangements are with your other family, thank you for coming to see him.'

'That's better. I remember that hot temper, but I'd hoped you'd got rid of it by now.'

Cherry knew he was baiting her and decided not to give in. She was only like this with him. It was such a pity that relationships which started out so lovingly should end in acrimony. Swallowing hard, she said, 'Jay's with friends at the moment, but I'm due to pick him up in an hour or so. Where are you staying?'

'Well, I shall stay here,' replied Alan. He put his arms around Cherry and murmured, 'I'm so sorry about the boat, I know how much it meant to you and Jay.'

When he spoke like that Cherry could remember why she'd married him. He hadn't changed completely, then. That was comforting.

'We've got staff accommodation now.' She shot him a watery smile. 'I could sleep in with Jay I suppose, or you could. What do you think?'

'I think it's better if I stay here. What about if I book a twin and then if Jay wants to stay with me, he can?'

Cherry took his arm and led him away from the desk. 'It's very pricey here, you know.'

'Do I look as if I count the pennies?' Alan asked, looking down at his Pierre Cardin suit.

Wondering uncharitably if they were his pennies or Imogen's, Cherry just said, 'Fine. Let's get you booked in, then I'll fetch Jay. He'll be so pleased to see you.' Knowing how true this was, Cherry added, 'Thank you for thinking of him, Alan.'

'That's one thing we always see eye to eye on, Cherry. Jay's a star!'

Sitting on her own in her cottage that evening, Cherry was happy for once. The look on Jay's face had been enough to tell her he was ecstatic to see his dad. She hadn't minded changing her plans of taking Jay bowling over the weekend. The fact that he was with his dad more than made up for anything she could have treated him to. Content to take a back seat, she'd got up to date with the ironing, baked some of Jay's favourite flapjacks and was now sitting out on the little patio wrapped in a fleecy jacket reading a thriller from the hotel library.

'Good evening, Cherry. Everything all right?' Oliver couldn't stop himself from looking for Cherry even though he told himself he was only getting some fresh air.

Looking up from her book, Cherry replied, 'Fine, Oliver. Do you want to come in for a cup of tea, glass of wine or something?'

Not sure if she was alone, Oliver felt uncomfortable. 'I don't want to interrupt anything,' he declared.

'I'm only reading.' She smiled. Now that Jay was happy, she felt a radiant glow about her. If only things could be that good with her and Oliver. She got up, closed the book and led him inside. Not sure what he'd like, she took a bottle of wine from the fridge, put the kettle on and laid out a plate of the newly baked flapjacks. They had turned out quite well, all sticky and soft with honey.

Uncorking the bottle, she indicated the plate and said, 'Help yourself. They're homemade, but nice all the same.' Her eyes shone teasingly.

'Thank you,' Oliver said, formally. 'Where do you find the time and energy to do all these things?'

'All what things?'

'Looking after Jay, working at the hotel, thinking up new ideas for the

153

hotel, baking . . . ' He was going to add and finding time to meet new men, but stopped himself as he knew it would sound petty.

'I suppose I wouldn't have done the baking if Jay had been around.' Cherry shrugged as she spoke.

'Where is he tonight? With Pat and her husband? He could have had another go on the computer. You were right, he is easy to get to know.' Then he blurted out, 'I wish I could say the same about his mother.'

Cherry looked at him in amazement. 'I'm not difficult to get on with, Oliver. Perhaps you don't want to get on with me.'

'What's the point? We have to have a working relationship, but that's all it can be, I understand that. Don't worry, Cherry, I won't try to cramp your style.' Oliver felt truly ashamed of himself. How could he be this mean to Cherry? If only he'd spoken to her before about his feelings, she mightn't have looked elsewhere.

Taking him by the arm, Cherry led him to the settee and sat down next to him. 'Oliver, what's going on?'

Letting out a breath, Oliver admitted, 'I saw you in reception. You were with someone. I didn't want to intrude. I was . . . ' He really wanted to say he was jealous, but there seemed little or no point in his confession now.

He looked surprised when Cherry burst out laughing. 'Oh Oliver, is that what's annoying you? I'm sorry if my behaviour wasn't proper in the public area, but it was my ex-husband, Alan. He turned up out of the blue and he seemed to think I'd be pleased to see him.'

'And were you?' Oliver asked, holding his breath waiting for her reply.

'Yes, of course I was.'

'I see,' said Oliver downing the remaining drops of wine from his glass. 'I'd better go.'

'You can't go yet, you haven't had any flapjack. Here, help yourself while I explain.'

Oliver sat back down on the settee and listened.

'I was pleased to see Alan because Jay would be so happy. He and Jay are spending the evening together. I haven't seen Jay as cheerful for a long while.' That wasn't true, reflected Cherry. He'd been equally as cheerful when Oliver had been showing him around the computer. But somehow she felt shy admitting that. While she'd been thinking of Jay, Oliver had placed his empty glass on the table and was pulling her towards him.

Holding her very gently, his mouth came down on hers and his fingers explored her hair and cheeks.

This time there was no mistaking his desire and Cherry responded to him with all her heart.

12

Cherry was pleased Oliver had called the previous Friday evening and she'd been able to explain about Alan although she still wasn't quite sure how he saw their relationship. However the air had been cleared and she hoped that when she arrived for work they would have the easygoing relationship they sometimes achieved when they were working together. Considering how little experience she had in the hotel business, she was surprised at how much notice Oliver took of her suggestions for the hotel. He'd given her complete freedom to design the brochure and she was very excited about her progress so far. Today she was going to take the photos and make a trip into town to the printers so that they could produce the proof. But first she needed to find a digital camera. It wasn't something she'd ever felt she and Jay had needed and she'd had to be careful with money since separating from Alan.

Before starting on the cleaning she decided to go to the office to see if Oliver had a camera she could use and she felt a need to see him and reassure herself that he was still the same Oliver she'd spent those precious intimate moments with. On entering the room she was disappointed to find him on the phone. He quickly finished the conversation with, 'I'll call you later,' but looked rather secretive, a bit like Jay when she'd caught him doing something she didn't approve of.

'Is everything all right, Oliver, you look a bit flushed.'

He mumbled, then shuffled a few papers on his desk.

'Good. I wanted to say how much Jay enjoyed spending time with you on the computer. He had great fun. Thanks.' She was getting no response. He looked engrossed in the paper he was holding.

She gave up. She just couldn't fathom him. Back to business then. 'I just wondered if you had a digital camera I could use. I'm hoping to take the photos.' She hoped he would suggest going with her. They could turn it into another outing. Just the two of them by the river, but this time she'd make sure he didn't get wet.

'Yes, here.' Oliver hurriedly reached into his desk and passed her the camera before busying himself again.

'Right, thanks.' Cherry realised things weren't back to normal between them and she was puzzled as to who could have been on the line to make him so distracted. She felt let down, but it was a lovely day and she decided to rearrange her timetable and head for the river to take a few pictures in the morning light.

Just as she approached the bank a sixty foot narrow boat chugged into view. Theirs had been a bit smaller, but very similar with the same traditional stern and a few small round windows.

She admired the colourful painted containers on the roof bursting with flowers and herbs. She'd had a small garden too and Jay had helped her care for the plants. She felt a lump in her throat and tears forming. She liked their cottage and knew they were very lucky, but the time they'd spent on the boat had seemed magical. It had been just her and Jay facing the world.

The woman at the helm waved at her and after Cherry had waved she took a few shots with the boat in the foreground. They were just the type she'd wanted. Slightly cheered she made her way back to the hotel ready to start cleaning the bedrooms.

As she passed reception she noticed a woman waiting at the desk. Cherry wondered if Oliver knew how much time Emma, the receptionist, was spending in the kitchen with Andre and how little time actually working.

'May I help,' she asked the attractive blonde, hoping she didn't look too scruffy, but knowing her hair was all over the place. She patted it frantically.

'I'm here to see Mr Fingle,' the woman replied with a gravelly voice. Cherry immediately assumed she must be a friend of Darius, probably an ex-girlfriend giving chase.

'I'm sorry, Darius has gone to Spain.'

'Not Darius, I'm here to see Olly.' The woman smiled, showing pearly white teeth.

Cherry smiled tightly back at the woman and asked her to take a seat while she called Oliver on the phone.

'There's someone to see you, but I think you were expecting her,' she hissed having suddenly realised why Oliver had been so embarrassed about the call he'd been making. Cherry was annoyed when he feigned surprise.

'Who is it?' he asked.

'Don't give me all that after giving me a hard time about Alan. Hypocrite!' She slammed the phone down and stamped off up the stairs. That morning she broke a cup in one of the bedrooms and cracked a toilet seat when she slammed it down. And she was very nearly rude to one of the guests who complained about the lack of a towelling dressing gown. Suddenly remembering she was now part of the management team she smiled sweetly, promised to bring one immediately and said she'd inform the owner of the hotel. If she ever spoke to him again, she added to herself.

She couldn't believe Oliver was doing this to her, letting her believe there was a possibility of a relationship with him and then meeting some other woman, right under her nose. But maybe he'd hoped the woman would be more discreet, maybe at least he'd wanted to break things to her gently. When she'd finished the cleaning she passed back through reception, but hurried down to the staff room when she saw Oliver and the woman sitting close together and laughing uproariously. Had she and Oliver ever laughed like that? She had a horrible feeling Oliver was holding the woman's hand.

Pat wasn't about so she wasn't able to give vent to her feelings. She ate her sandwiches and drank her tea and began to feel less and less angry and more and more upset. For the first time since her split from Alan she'd met a man she really cared for. But just what were her feelings for Oliver? He made her heart beat fast, made her emotions dance ... The truth was she'd fallen in love with him. And now he was going to let her down. Well, she'd steer clear of men for the rest of her life. Banging the lid back on to her sandwich box she prepared to get back to work, but just at that moment Emma floated in bringing a hint of jasmine with her. She had a dreamy look and Cherry wondered whether she should throw a glass of cold water over her to bring her back to reality.

'Do you believe in love at first sight?' Emma asked languorously.

Cherry wasn't sure she believed in love at all any more and said nothing.

'The first time I saw Andre I was

smitten. It happened to him too. Can you believe it? Have you ever been deeply in love?'

Cherry didn't answer immediately. She'd thought she'd loved Alan, but she didn't want to delve into her feelings for Oliver. 'I've been married,' she said dodging the question.

'We're going to get married. As soon as we've told our families and arranged things. How long will that take? I can't wait. Do you think Oliver will give us a reduction if we hold the wedding here?' Emma's eyes sparkled.

'Who'll do the cooking? Andre?'

Emma laughed. 'You're really funny. It's no wonder Oliver fancies you.'

Cherry hadn't meant to be funny, she was too upset to be humorous, but Emma's comment had intrigued her. 'What d'you mean about Oliver fancying me?'

'Don't tell me you haven't noticed. We're always laughing about it. In a nice way, we think he's cute. He's always gazing at you with a soppy look.

Wandering round the hotel when you're cleaning hoping he'll bump into you. All the staff know he's crazy about you. We thought you were getting quite friendly with each other.'

For an instant Cherry glowed, but then she remembered the secret phone call and the woman who called him Olly. 'I think you must all have it wrong,' she said.

Emma shrugged and resumed gazing dreamily into space.

★   ★   ★

Cherry felt that she ought to go to the office for the afternoon, but once again wondered whether or not she was doing the right thing working so closely with someone she had such strong feelings for. She really didn't want to be in close proximity to Oliver right now so she decided to take the camera and get some more pictures. That could be called working, surely, not that it mattered any more.

Having walked in the woods, taken pictures of everything that appealed to her, including the intricate patterns in the bark of some of the trees, she headed back to the river. The sky was darkening and she hoped for some dramatic shots. Lying on the ground trying to catch a last shaft of sunlight piercing the foliage of a tree she suddenly understood how challenging the new job would have been. She'd have to resign even though it was just the sort of work she needed both mentally and financially. She closed her eyes and wondered why things never quite worked out for her. Suddenly she felt huge drops of rain falling on her face. She rushed to stand up and shelter under the tree, but the rain was torrential and soon even the cover of the leaves wasn't enough to protect her and she was soaked. Her blouse clung to her and looking down she saw it was now pretty much see-through. Checking her watch she realised Jay would be back from school. She'd have to nip back to the hotel hoping not to be spotted, change into her overalls and meet Jay. She didn't intend working any more today and she'd have to give her future some serious thought.

As she entered the hotel car park Oliver was escorting the woman to her car, his huge black umbrella sheltering her completely from the rain. Cherry couldn't possibly appear now so hid behind the nearest car. Peering over the bonnet she could see the two of them quite clearly. Even if Oliver wasn't interested in her she still didn't want to be compared to the immaculate woman stepping gracefully into her sleek car. Her own hair hung down in dripping rats' tails and her feet squelched in her shoes. She was starting to feel shivery and wished they'd hurry up with their goodbyes. She couldn't resist watching the goodbye. It was nothing more than a peck on the cheek, but maybe Oliver was being careful in case a member of staff saw him. At last he'd waved her off and was making his way to the main door. Cherry sneaked round the back and through the staff entrance where she bumped straight into Oliver.

'What on earth?' he asked.

'I've been working, taking photos for the brochure. Here,' she said, 'take this. You'll have to download the photos and go to the printers tomorrow. I've had enough for today, in fact I'm resigning.' She nearly burst into tears, but knew she had to collect herself ready to find Jay. She rushed to the staff room only then remembering her see-through blouse. No wonder Oliver had looked aghast.

* * *

Having been home with Jay, showered and changed, Cherry felt slightly better, but in need of some company. Jay had jumped at the chance of calling in to see Maurice and telling him about Mahjong.

'You don't look yourself,' Pat said to Cherry ushering her into the cosy

168

kitchen. 'We'll let the others have the sitting room and we can have a good chat.' She busied herself filling the kettle and putting coffee in mugs whilst Cherry sat at the table and said nothing. 'What is it then? You might as well tell me now you're here.'

'I've fallen in love . . . '

'That's not news. I know that. You two could do with having your heads knocked together.

'We all know. You can't keep secrets in a hotel. So what's happened?'

'The trouble is he keeps giving me different messages. One minute I think he likes me and the next he doesn't seem to care for me at all and is seeing another woman.' Cherry was determined not to break down.

'That's not possible!' Pat was shocked. 'He wouldn't do that.'

'I saw her at the hotel. They seemed very close and comfortable together. And he was embarrassed when I caught him talking on the phone to her just before she turned up.'

'I still don't believe it, he's not that sort of man. He just wouldn't do it. Anyway he's crazy about you. Any opportunity he has he talks about you, wants to know if I've seen you, where you are, what you're doing, if you're all right and happy.'

'Really?' Cherry was amazed. 'But who was the woman?'

'Do you know what I think? The best thing would be to go and talk to him, ask him a few questions and get some answers. It's ridiculous carrying on like this when you could be enjoying being with each other. Why not go now? We'll see to Jay. And if you're late I'll walk him home, see him to bed and wait until you get back.'

Tears welled in Cherry's eyes. 'You're such a good friend. I couldn't manage without you.' She stood up and went over to give her friend a hug. 'I won't go now, but tomorrow I'll see Oliver. I told him I was resigning, but now I don't know what to do.'

'Don't even think about it. Wait until

you see what he says. You're indispensable. Everyone likes you, you cheer the place up.'

Cherry knew Pat's advice was sensible and she resolved to try to have a good night's sleep so that she could be strong when she faced Oliver the next day.

★ ★ ★

The following morning she found Oliver in reception huddled over a pot of strong coffee looking much the worse for wear. He was unshaven and wearing the same clothes she'd last seen him in. On seeing her his face lit up, but then remembering her words of the previous day it fell again.

'So you're back to hand in your notice?' he asked barely looking at her.

'I'm here to talk to you, Oliver,' she said sitting next to him, taking the solitary cup and gulping down the scalding liquid. 'I'm not sure about anything right now. Sometimes I think you like me and sometimes you can barely speak to me. When I caught you on the phone yesterday you . . .'

'Sssh,' Oliver said placing his finger to her lips. 'Let me explain.'

He took her hand and cradled it briefly before bringing it to his own lips. Just feeling his mouth brush her hand ever so gently made her all a quiver.

There were so many questions she needed to ask. 'I can't keep quiet, Oliver. You were put out when you saw me with Alan, but then yesterday you were with another woman and you looked so close.'

'You were jealous? That was Rebecca, you know about her. She's happily married with twin girls. We're still very fond of each other, but that's it.' He ran his hands through his hair and said, 'But she annoys the hell out of me when she calls me 'Olly'.' Suddenly his eyes twinkled. 'You didn't have to reveal yourself to get my attention!'

Cherry blushed, then laughed. 'It

wasn't intentional. I'd been out in the rain working.'

'Ah, yes, work. Are you still intent on resigning? I thought we had a future together, here at the hotel. It was going to be so vibrant and exciting, but I can't do it on my own. I need you.'

She still didn't know what he meant. Did he simply want her to work at the hotel or did he need her to love him, be his partner in every possible area of their lives.

'As for the phone call. That was all to do with something I need to show you. It's a big surprise I've been planning. But Jay must come too. It's for him as well.'

'He's at school until three, can't we see it without him?' Cherry felt mean, but was desperate to find out what this was all about.

'Definitely not. You'll have to be patient and wait.' With that Oliver kissed her quickly on the lips and left.

Cherry gritted her teeth. She'd so hoped she'd know where she stood by now. Just then Pat breezed through reception. 'Come on, Cherry, six bedrooms have been vacated and need cleaning. But first, tell me the latest about you and Oliver.'

★ ★ ★

Cherry didn't have a good day, but she managed to finish her cleaning and work in the office. Thankfully Oliver wasn't about, only appearing miraculously when Jay arrived home from school.

'Ready Cherry?' he asked, grinning. 'Come on, let's go.' As they left the building he took their hands and led them towards the river. Cherry couldn't imagine what they were going to see. As they drew closer to the river Jay exclaimed, 'There's a boat on one of your moorings!'

'I'm so pleased for you,' Cherry said politely. She tried to sound pleased, but was disappointed that Oliver thought this was a good surprise for them. In fact it made her feel sad again because the roof of the boat, the only part they could see, looked very much like their boat, *Dream Maker*.

Jay suddenly pulled his hand out of Oliver's and ran to the boat shouting, 'It is, it is!'

Oliver gripped Cherry's hand firmly and started running with her.

'Look Mum, it's *Dream Maker*,' Jay called back before leaping on to the boat to investigate. By the time Oliver and a breathless Cherry had reached it Jay had disappeared into the cabin.

'It's yours,' Oliver said proudly, 'yours and Jay's. I had it restored and refitted. I know how much it means to you both, but you seem happy in the cottage, so it's up to you. You can do what you like with it, live on it, hire it out, use it for holidays.'

Cherry was speechless so Oliver took the opportunity to kiss her firmly on the mouth. This time it wasn't a snatched kiss, but long and lingering, making her insides melt and her heart pound against her chest. Cherry wrapped her arms around him and responded with ever-growing passion.

'Ugh, you're not going to have a baby are you?' Jay giggled poking his head out of one of the windows.

Hearing his voice, Cherry guiltily tried to spring apart from Oliver, but his grip on her was firm. He wasn't letting her go anywhere. When he was ready he lifted his head and said, 'Now that's not a bad idea, Jay, but maybe not just yet.' The two adults watched Jay disappear back inside.

'So what do you say, Cherry? Do we have a future together? I'm always so excited at the thought of seeing you or hearing your voice. I couldn't bear it if you walked away from me. Please Cherry, stay with me, I love you and I want to be with you. I want to know everything about you both. Do you think there's room for three of us on the *Dream Maker*?'

Although Cherry didn't say a word, Oliver was left in no doubt as to what her answer would be when she eventually decided to speak.

Other titles in the
Linford Romance Library:

THE POWER AND THE PASSION

Joyce Johnson

After a failed business venture and a broken engagement, artist Abbie Richards takes advantage of an opportunity to do a year's English teaching in Sicily. There, she becomes involved with the large, extended Puzzi family; its members wealthy and powerfully placed in the community. Abbie enjoys the teaching and the social life at Maria Puzzi's language school, and falls in love with charismatic surgeon Roberto Puzzi, only to find herself dangerously entangled in the Puzzi power struggles . . .